"Earthlings"
by Frick Weber

For my fellow daydreamers,

1. PROJECTILE

"Tell me child, what do you remember?" the jagged voice asked.

Slowly the darkness began to fade. Then light and blurred images began to emerge, and with them came memories. "I . . . I remember . . . not wanting to go fishing," answered Edison, and then he remembered more. "I usually get seasick, and it really sucks that I have to work on my foster family's fishing boat. They're not bad, but they go a bit overboard, no pun intended, on the whole character building experience of working the Great Lakes. I have to take like three showers to get rid of the fish stink." Edison tried to stretch, and wanted to rub his foggy eyes, but he couldn't move. His arms were bound to his sides. Not by belts, something much scratchier, maybe fraying ropes, or even vines . . . if that was possible?

"The day child, what else do you remember of the day?"

"Uh . . . the boat was full. Saturdays in the summertime usually are. Mainly older people, bunch of guys from some VFW, they all wore old navy hats. One guy had a big tattoo of a submarine with a shark mouth and tail on his arm . . . U.S.S. something or other. And there was a family . . . mom, dad, grandma, and two girls. The older girl had really long pretty blonde hair, like a model. I think she might have been fifteen or fourteen, a year older than me. I don't think she wanted to go fishing either, and she had an awkward, stumpy looking little sister, she could have been adopted."

"Gee thanks," said a young girl.

"Huh?" said Edison. The voice sounded like it was directly behind him. He tried to turn his head, but his body wouldn't move. Even if he'd been free, his vision was still too blurred for him to see anything or anyone. The darkness that clouded his sight slowly faded to earthly hues of green and brown.

"The boat, child. Do you remember what happened to the boat?" asked the jagged voice.

"Um, it . . . I saw . . . uh."

"What, what did you see?" the jagged voice grew excited.

Edison shut his eyes tight in an effort to help squeeze out the memory. "I tried to talk to the pretty blonde girl, but I don't think I made a good first impression?"

"Oh, 'ya think!" said the young girl's voice.

"Huh?"

"Hush girl. The boat, child . . . what happened to the boat?" Impatience surfaced in the voice. The image of a dark brown blur took a step closer, it belonged to the jagged voice.

"I went over to see if I could help bait the girls' hooks, but the pretty one wasn't fishing. She was laying back and trying to tan. And that's when I realized how choppy the water was. Because when I went to say hello, I kind of threw up on her. A lot." The young female voice behind Edison gave a small laugh. "She started screaming and I ran to the back of the boat. And then her mother started screaming, and her grandmother, and then my foster dad, I think? I was kind of busy throwing up over the back of the boat. While I was ah . . . feeding the fish, I noticed the water current behind the boat had changed direction. Something was pulling the water back." He paused, "that's when I looked up, and saw it. The wave." Edison could feel the girl behind him shiver. "It was huge . . . and rolling straight toward the boat. When it hit, it must have looked like someone dropped a football stadium on a matchbox car. And then everything went black."

"Is that all you saw?" the brown blur took a step closer.

"Yeah."

"Good, good child."

Edison could feel the dank warmth of the brown blur's breath on his face. It smelled like dirt, and made his nose itch. He tried to wiggle an arm free of his bonds, but it was no use. They seemed to grow tighter when he moved. As Edison's vision cleared, the talking brown blur looked more like a ground hog standing on its hind legs than it did a person. While he couldn't exactly see whom the jagged voice belonged to, he could tell it was smiling. The blur gave a satisfied nod, walked over to a tree, and tugged on a vine. Edison's body moved as the blurry figure moved the vine. Edison squinted, the blur looked like a garden gnome covered in mud, no . . . not mud . . . vines? Its body was made out of a mesh of brown vines and roots. The young girl behind Edison wiggled her body, and stretched her neck.

"Is there someone tied to my back?"

"Yep," answered the little root man as he walked over to a tree on the opposite side of Edison, and tugged on another vine. Edison's body bounced. He looked down at the rigging he was suspended in. It hung between two tall trees.

"And is this . . . a slingshot?"

"Hmmm . . . actually, it's more of a catapult."

"Catapult?"

"Yep." The root man picked up a loose vine that was lying on the grass in front of Edison. "What is that phrase you fleshies use . . . God Speed?"

WHOOOOOOSSSSSSSSHHHHHHHH!

Edison, and the young girl tied to his back, screamed as they were catapulted into the air.

2. BREEZES

Edison had never flown on an airplane before, so he really didn't have anything to compare this flight to. From his limited point of view, the ascent was quite peaceful. As the wind blew through his unkempt hair, he felt as if he were sitting in the back seat of a convertible, driving down a country road on a warm summer day.

The island below him shrank as they flew up, out, and over the dark water of Lake Superior. It was an island he was unfamiliar with, and he was familiar with all of the islands on the lake. The island was actually submerged below the water's surface. From this height, Edison thought the island looked like it was at the bottom of a hole. And it appeared to be growing, as the water around the shore pulled away. Surrounding the submerged island, approximately forty yards off its shoreline was a waterfall ring. The shallow waters around the island seemed to open up like a giant trough or moat. As the water drained away, the lush green island revealed itself. There was a clearing on one side of the island that was speckled with stone ruins, and scattered across eighty percent of the island were the tall peaks of a dense jungle. A small mountain rose in the center. And along the south shore, Edison saw what he thought was his foster family's fishing boat, teetering back and forth on top of a tree. But he wasn't quite sure . . . for that was when the descent began.

If the ascent was smooth and comforting, the descent was the complete opposite. Edison tried to scream, but his voice was stolen as his lungs collapsed in on themselves. They were so high, and the drop was so long he thought they would suffocate before they hit the water. The girl tied to his back went rigid. Their bodies howled through the wind like cannonballs whooshing toward a target. With an endless landscape of dark, cold water below them, it was impossible to tell how high they really were. Edison forgot the island, forgot the pretty blonde girl, forgot her awkward little sister, and also forgot the little, brown gnome made of roots. The shock and awe of the moment seemed to stretch on for an eternity. And then they landed. There was an explosion, and for the second time that day, everything went black. SPLASH!

3. POP

Edison once heard about a man named Kevin. He wasn't able to remember the man's last name until after he hit the water. SPLASH. Hines, Kevin Hines. Edison found Kevin's story particularly relevant during his fall. Kevin Hines jumped off San Francisco's Golden Gate Bridge. Hitting the water from that height was supposed to be like hitting cement. In this particular story, the man who jumped from the 25-story tall bridge survived, and he credited his survival to vertical entry. He made his body straight like an arrow, and broke the surface of the water with his pointing toes. Edison figured, that was what he must have done, unintentionally of course. Because he could feel his stomach inflating and water surging all around his body as he sank.

The deeper they sank, the darker it got. And it got very dark. Their bodies remained upright as they sank. After a couple of long minutes, the kind of minutes one would experience while waiting for a pot of water to boil, their dive ended. Edison felt his feet hit the sandy clay bottom of the lake. He then realized he must be almost a foot taller than the girl tied to his back, since it took a few moments for her feet to touch the bottom. As she slid down behind Edison, the water soaked vines binding the two gave way, and Edison was finally free to scratch the itch on his nose.

Edison's tense limbs began to hurt, and his puffed checks trembled as they begged him to release the air trapped within. A small wave of panic sent a shiver through his body as he kicked off, and paddled for the faint hazy glow of the surface above. He didn't get very far. A small hand tightened around his ankle, and four sharp nails dug into his boney shin. He looked down and saw the awkward little sister of the pretty, blonde girl standing on the bottom of the lake. She didn't look happy. Edison was yanked down. At the same time that his feet hit the clay lake bottom, a tiny fist struck Edison right in the gut. BLUB! The precious air trapped in his cheeks broke free.

A softball-sized bubble shot out of his mouth and two smaller, gumball-sized bubbles shot out of his nose. They joined and tripled in size, then tripled again, and again, and again. At the age of four, Edison learned about the directional flow of bubbles under water, through filling up squirt guns in the dirty buckets of rainwater on the farm of his third foster family. The bubbles were supposed to travel upwards to the surface, but this bubble, now the size of a Volkswagen Beetle, did not travel up. Instead the growing bubble floated down to rest on the dark floor of the lake. Edison stared in frozen wonder, as the awkward little girl walked toward the bubble. She yanked Edison along behind her, the way a child would pull a balloon.

"Holy crap! Did I do that!" Edison landed with a soft soggy thump inside the bubble. "Did you see that? Are we at the bottom of the lake? What is this? We can breathe. Can we breathe?" Edison took two giant and very deep breaths. "Is this air? Did I do this? How did I do this?" Edison stopped talking, his nose twitched, and he recoiled as he caught a whiff of a foul odor. "Oh man, what is that?"

"Well, if I were to take a guess . . . burp and scrambled eggs. What did you have for breakfast?"

"Uh, scrambled eggs with cheese."

"There you go, burp and eggs. And yes . . . you did do this," the young girl spread her arms and motioned toward the large bubble surrounding them.

"Cool."

"It would have been cooler if you had brushed your teeth."

"Sorry, I slept in and was running late." The awkward little sister of the beautiful, blondee girl turned and faced Edison. She stood with her hands on her hips, dripping water. They were both drenched. Edison noticed she had short dark hair unlike her sister and she wore a long sleeve dark brown shirt and navy blue shorts. This sister was not as awkward looking as he originally thought. She was still awkward, but in more of a quiet bookworm way. "Hi."

"Awkward, huh?"

"Ah, yeah . . . sorry about that, I kind of didn't know you were tied to my back."

"No kidding. And don't worry about it," she turned and added underneath her breath, "I've been called worse."

"Sorry again, uh . . ." Edison sat up as the awkward little sister of the beautiful, blonde girl slowly turned around. He stuck out his hand to shake. "I'm Edison."

"Yeah I know, I'm Ellie," she smiled sheepishly as they shook hands. "So what do people call you? Ed? Eddie?"

"Uh, nothing I'd really like to repeat." Ellie held her gaze tightly, and seemed to look deep into his eyes. She smiled, and he quickly turned away. "Uh hey, uh . . . do you know how we . . . you . . . I . . . me?" He pointed up and around.

"The bubble?"

"Yeah," Edison nodded.

"Hmpf, well . . . you did it, but I guess, in a round about way, that's kind of my fault. Sorry." The apology was an awkward moment for Ellie. And while it may have taken an extra 10 or 12 cubic square inches of horsepower for her to speak the "S-word" the exhaustive effort went completely unnoticed.

A look of panic overtook Edison's face, and he jumped to his feet. "Oh man, we've got to get to the surface! We're gonna suffocate! There can't be much air in here. We're gonna RUN OUT! We're gonna . . ."

Edison reached out his hand to break the surface of the bubble, as Ellie grabbed him by the collar of his t-shirt, and yanked him back. "We can't! Not yet . . . we have to wait."

"Wait, wait for what? We're gonna die!"

Ellie motioned for Edison to shush, and quietly pointed up. It only took Edison a moment to see it.

The faint hazy glow of the surface began to wipe away, as large objects slowly crept past. Creaks, scrapes, and cracks echoed and reverberated through the murky water's depths, as small flecks and shards rained down on the bubble. Edison peered up at one of the larger flecks that landed on top of the bubble. "Is that . . ."

"Ice. Those are the Ice Giants."

The creaks, scrapes, and cracks grew louder, and stronger as the murky-green glow of the surface gave way to darkness. Edison and Ellie took a step toward each other. The only comfort the darkness had to offer was when they would occasionally bump into each other. A signal that let them know they were not alone. It was a complete and perfect blackness, void of any and

11

all light. The only other time Edison experienced such darkness was when two of the older boys at his fifth foster family's house tied him up in old comforters, stuffed him under the steps in the basement, and turned out the lights. To date, those were the longest and loneliest two hours of his life. At least that time there was the sound of giggling pranksters. This time there was only the terrifying moans and groans of the giant ice behemoths sliding above.

CRACK. The sound rang out like a menacing crack of lightening. It was so close Edison jumped and cringed, as Ellie sank ten small nails into his right arm. The darkness shifted, as a fissure in the ice formed, and a small sliver of light crept down from the surface. Edison and Ellie gasped. Inches above the top of the bubble, and far too close for comfort, was a seemingly endless field of jagged ice spikes. Edison quickly realized that Mr. Hermphner, his sixth grade science teacher, was right. Ninety percent of the mass of an iceberg does in fact lie just below the surface, and at the moment, right above their heads. Then, as quickly as the cleft in the ice opened, it closed. And with it went the light it brought, and what little sense of comfort it had offered.

The eight minutes of darkness that followed felt like an eternity. Slowly the dim haze of the surface returned, and Edison was able to see Ellie's face once more. She looked off at the trailing icebergs with intense interest. Edison hated silence, so naturally he was the first to break it. "So ah, now what?"

Ellie calmly turned to Edison and smiled, "Now . . . it's your turn."

"MY TURN! What do you . . ."

Ellie sucked in a deep breath, motioned for him to do the same, grabbed his hand tightly, extended her free hand to the bubble wall, and flicked it. POP!

4. SUBMERGED

Behind the curtain of a dense wall of fog, and hidden from the rest of the world, the icebergs sailed on toward the submerged island. A phenomenal site, too bad the only ones to bare witness to it were a thirteen-year-old boy and a twelve-year-old girl.

"Gasp!"

They broke the surface. Edison wiped the excess water from his face, and Ellie pulled several wet locks of hair from her forehead. "Wow." The iceberg was now a hundred yards away, and gently inched closer to the submerged island. It stood like a crystal cathedral on the water's surface, and in comparison, Edison and Ellie looked like nothing more than dormice.

"So, what was it we needed to do?" asked Edison.

"Well, that is an Ice Giant, and he . . . or she . . . it actually . . . is headed to the island. And when it gets there, it's going to kill everyone on the boat," said Ellie.

"And how do you know that?"

"Twig told me. He's the little root man that catapulted us out here . . . he's our friend," answered Ellie. Had Edison been a better listener, or even just a tad bit less spellbound, he might have been surprised by Ellie's matter-of-fact tone. Ellie was one of those rare people who reacted conversely to the world around her. The crazier things got around her, the calmer she became. At the age of seven, her family's annual "family-pumpkin-patch-portrait" turned into a baby calf, petting zoo stampede. And while the first wet snout had sent her sister Vivian into hysterics, Ellie calmly reacted to restore order to the unbalanced world around her. Internally, the gears of her mind spun to analyze the building chaos and devised a plan to restore order and defuse the current predicament. She grabbed her sister's Prom Queen Princess doll, threw it at the legs of a nearby feeding trough, cracked the doll's face, spilled a small mountain of seed, and stemmed the half-pint stampede. The crisis had been averted moments after it started. However, this personality trait also had its downside. Take something like a kid's birthday party. While everyone else ran around yelling and having fun, Ellie tended to fade into the corner like a wallflower, not really knowing how to "join in."

"You want to stop THAT?" asked Edison. Ellie nodded. "Yeah, let me know how that goes."

"Oh . . . no, not me . . . you." Ellie bobbed up and down, as they treaded water. She wasn't a very strong swimmer, and it took a lot of effort for her to talk and stay afloat.

"Me?" Edison turned and gave Ellie the classic "are-you-crazy look" and in return received a simple smile. "What do you want me to do, burp a bubble at them?"

"No, I don't think that would do it. Twig told me you could do just about anything with water. So I was thinking . . ."

"Who's Twig? And what do I do with water?" asked Edison.

"I already told you . . . *huff* . . . Twig was the little rooty guy who catapulted us out here," said Ellie as she struggled to stay afloat.

"Rooty guy?"

"Yeah, he's made of roots. At first I thought he was made of vines . . . *huff* . . . but when you look closely, it's pretty obvious they're roots. But that's not important now."

"I do stuff with water?"

"Yeah, bunches of stuff. *Huff.* And so we . . ."

"How?' Edison quickly cut her off.

"That's not really important right now either. Look, the iceberg is almost to . . . *huff* . . . the waterfall ring," said Ellie. "We need to think of . . . *huff* . . . got it. A wave. Edison . . . *huff* . . . think of a wave."

Edison's only response was a blink. The lights may have been on, but no one was home. His mouth opened and closed several times but nothing came out. Ellie was no stranger to this look of bewilderment. Most exchanges with her older sister Vivian ended this way. She quickly took control of the situation. She grabbed Edison by the arm, and turned him toward the iceberg. She went under for a moment, but with a good kick of her legs quickly bounced back up to the surface. "Think wave, Woosh!" She pointed and then spread her arms toward the iceberg.

"Woosh?"

14

"Wave! Think of a BIG WAVE . . . *huff* . . . shooting though the water and . . . *huff* . . . HITTING the icebergs." It was getting harder for Ellie to tread water.

"A wave?'

"Just DO IT!"

Edison winced as Ellie slapped the water. She bobbed under again.

"Are you OK . . ."

Ellie came up growling and glaring. Edison quickly turned and looked toward the pack of traveling icebergs. He closed his eyes, and thought of a wave. It didn't feel like much, so he opened his eyes, as an apology formed on his wet lips. Ellie's face was the first thing he noticed, and she no longer looked mad. In fact, her face was a swirl of wonder and approval. He turned toward the icebergs.

Halfway between Edison and the iceberg was a three-foot ripple of water. No white caps, but a wave nonetheless. The wave hit the back of an iceberg, and tilted the frozen mammoth ever so slightly. "Great job Edison . . . *huff, huff*." Ellie patted him on the back, and in doing so, bobbed under, "*Blub*!" She popped to the surface, full of support and enthusiasm. "Now this time . . . *huff* . . . think of a big torpedo slicing through the water . . . *blub* . . . and smashing into it!"

"Torpedo?"

"Yeah, a really fast one. And give a . . . *huff* . . . do a big splash with your hands." Edison repeated Ellie's words to himself several times, and practiced a few small splashing gestures with his hands. "Yeah, like your pushing it!" coached Ellie.

Edison nodded, and thought to himself. *What the heck, they just spent ten minutes underwater in a bubble he burped, why not a water-torpedo.* He closed his eyes, and started the countdown. *Five, four, three, two, ONE!*

Edison's face tensed, he gritted his teeth, and pushed his hands through the water toward the giant iceberg. This time he felt it. It was a like a giant gust of air sweeping through him. It came out of nowhere, and sped past as quickly as it appeared. Ellie's jaw dropped open. She grabbed his shoulder in excitement and to keep from bobbing under. She did not want to miss the impact. Edison opened his eyes. Surprise was clearly the theme of the day.

It took seconds for the water torpedo to close the distance. And as it slammed into the back of the iceberg, a rumble of thunder echoed underwater. It raised Edison a foot out of the water. He could feel the impact a hundred yards away. A reverberating ripple sped past him and bobbed Ellie under. CRACK! The back of the largest iceberg split. A huge chunk of ice slowly fell away, and slid under the surface. Drifts of snow and chunks of ice fell down into the water. And for a brief moment, Edison thought he saw a face in the ice staring back at him. It was a very confused face, with two wounded and sad-puppy-dog-like-eyes.

"Quick, do it again! *Huff* . . . we can't let it reach the island!"

Edison blinked away the image of the wounded ice face, and closed his eyes. He imagined a bigger, faster water torpedo. And with gritted teeth, he pushed out with both hands as hard as he could. He opened his eyes and saw two huge jet streams shooting through the water in front of him. The icebergs tried to move to the right in an effort to dodge the attack. But they were much too big, and too slow to avoid the oncoming blast. There were two explosions, one right after the other, which were followed by a dozen cracks and five times as many splashes. Water fell from the sky like a quick summer shower at the beach. If the giant icebergs at one time resembled a cathedral, all but the altar splintered and fell away. The ice face returned and this time Ellie saw it too. It was round and old, the kind you might expect to see in the knotted trunk of a three hundred year old tree. That is of course, if trees had faces. And it was sad and in pain. As quickly as it had appeared, it was gone. The last of the icebergs slid down below the surface.

Edison and Ellie didn't celebrate their victory.

17

5. FOUND

With Ellie's help, it took Edison about twenty minutes to gain control over his new abilities. By concentrating and visualizing on the task, Edison was able to keep them both afloat, and moving through the water. A good thing for Ellie, who figured she had already swallowed three gallons of lake water, and was four or five short minutes away from drowning. Other than the mental strain, Edison showed no signs of fatigue. On any other day he would have been exhausted, especially since he was a bad swimmer. But today was different. And every minute was filled with something amazing. Giant life sustaining burp bubbles, summertime icebergs in Lake Superior, powerful water-torpedoes, talking clumps of roots, sunken green islands, a giant waterfall ring, and the ability to control water.

Edison's new abilities were a fascinating mystery to him. But every time Edison tried to discuss it with Ellie, who seemed to know a little bit more about it than he did, he would lose his concentration and Ellie would slip under the water. BLUB. BLUB. Edison tried talking about Ellie's sister Vivian. BLUB. BLUB. Edison tried talking about the big wave. BLUB. BLUB. He tried talking about Ellie's sister again. BLUB. BLUB. Ellie gave him a good punch as she bobbed under the water. Edison's effort at keeping them afloat was similar to that of a newborn trying to walk. Their progress was slow and tiring. But it was a wondrously new event, ripe with promise and unlimited possibilities. Ellie was a great crutch for Edison. Without her, he would have made little or no progress at all.

The sun was slowly beginning to set, and it gave them a greater sense of urgency to return to the island. The eastern sky slowly darkened, while the western horizon faded to amber. It reminded Edison of something he'd often heard Captain Ralph, his sixth and current foster father, say, "Red at night, sailor's delight. Red at morn, sailor's scorn." Either way, both Edison and Ellie were deep in thought and neither noticed the growing roar of the rushing water. "Ahhhhhhhhhhhhh!"

The submerged island was invisible on the horizon, and had snuck up on them rather quickly. Without warning, the two

would-be-sailors flew out over the falls, and into thin air.
Initially, Edison didn't think that the waterfall ring looked very
high. He was wrong. With much screaming, flailing and kicking
they plummeted like lead weights. The only thought he had as
his lungs collapsed was . . . *ROCKS!* A faceless voice from the
past snickered, *it wasn't the fall that killed him, IT WAS THE
ROCKS!* He closed his eyes and screamed some more.

The roar of the falls was deafening, and the fall seemed to
last forever. So long, in fact, that Edison must have gotten used
to it as air returned to inflate his lungs. And at some point, both
Ellie and Edison had even stopped screaming. Fear soon gave
way to curiosity, and Edison slowly opened one of his tightly
clenched eyes, but only just a hair. He saw Ellie. She wasn't
screaming, and she wasn't falling. She was just kind of sitting
there, in a large glob of water. The glob looked like a bathtub of
water, but without the tub. Edison opened his other eye. Ellie
leaned over and said something to Edison, and even though he
was trying to listen, he couldn't hear a word she said. The roar of
the falls thundered all around them. Ellie even reached out her
hand to feel the spray of the falling water. *How curious*, the
young girl thought.

They floated to the bottom of the falls, hovering three feet
above the lowered surface in a giant glob of suspended water.
And if the surface of Lake Superior represented sea level, the
sunken green island sat four hundred feet below that. The
shoreline was less than a hundred feet away, a manageable swim
for even Ellie.

"Did I . . . ?" Edison was at a loss for words. Burp
bubbles, water torpedoes, and now floating bathtubs of water.
Ellie turned and looked at him. She was grinning ear to ear, and
her eyes were staring deep into Edison's.

"You're freak'n awesom-"

Edison blushed, lost concentration, and they both fell
down into the water. After a few submerged seconds, they
splashed to the surface spitting and coughing up water. They
looked up at the falls and then inspected their bodies for broken
limbs. Finding no injuries, they looked at each other, laughed,
and then hugged. Surprisingly, there was no undercurrent from
the falls. The raging water seemed to tuck down, into, and under

the wall of water surrounding the island. The water around the island was calm, like the still pools of a fairy-tale lagoon. And the submerged green island, with its lush vegetation, ancient ruins, and rocky outcroppings was something magical.

"Twig. Twig!" Ellie was the first one to shore, and she ran up to the green edge of what looked like a tropical rain forest. "We did it! Twig!" She looked around, and bit her lip. While at thirteen years of age, Edison had practically no experience deciphering the many mixed signals that girls projected, even he could tell something was wrong. "Twig?"

"Maybe we're at the wrong-"

"He told me to meet him at the giant turtle."

"Well, I don't see-"

Ellie spun Edison around and pointed to a small mound at the edge of the forest. Edison squinted, and saw the head of a giant stone turtle half-buried in the sand. The head was taller than him, and the small mound was actually the moss-covered shell of the giant stone tortoise. "Wow, that's pretty big." A few of the thin trees next to one of the turtle's feet started to rustle.

"Twig!" Ellie took off running toward the tree line, and then froze in her tracks. Directly in front of her, and sprinting out of the jungle was a tall, thin tree. It ran on a stout pair of root legs. And with branches for arms, it reached for Ellie. Edison screamed, and ran off into water, leaving Ellie to fend for herself. *So much for chivalry,* Ellie thought. She had no time to run, and the tall, thin tree was on her in seconds. "Ahhhh mmmmffff–" The tall thin tree grabbed Ellie with its limbs and muffled her mouth. Edison kept running into the water, screaming like a banshee.

"Hush small carbonite, it is not safe. You mustn't let them hear you!" spoke the tall, thin tree. The tree's words immediately silenced Ellie, who blinked in disbelief. After talking with a clump of roots, she didn't think a talking tree would faze her that much, but it did. The tall tree frantically looked around the beach, desperate to make sure they had not been heard. "Where is your companion going?"

Ellie turned and saw that Edison was still screaming and running wildly through the water. "Yeah, he's not really the

20

bravest – ouuf!" The tall, thin tree scooped up Ellie and sprinted off after Edison.

Edison glanced back over his shoulder and saw that the tree, having already captured Ellie, was now coming for him. He thought nothing of the floating water globs, torpedoes, or burp bubbles. All he could do was scream and run. The sound of his screams only made the tree run faster, and with more urgency. Edison turned back again, and got smacked in the face with a mesh of branches. He was yanked up out of the water and turned upside down.

"Oh hey, thanks for ditching me back there," said Ellie.

"I think this tree is alive," whispered Edison.

"Oh gee, ya' think?"

"Alive, I most certainly–," added the tall, thin tree.

"Ahhhhhhhh!" Edison screamed again. The tree panicked. And not knowing what else to do, it shoved Edison under the water to silence his scream. BLUUBBBB!

The tall thin tree turned to Ellie, and looked at her like she was the owner of a puppy who had just pooped in his yard. "My word, does he always carry on like this?"

"The whole talking tree thing is kind of new to him . . . me too actually."

"Well I'd say, carrying on like this, why would any tree want to talk with him?" Ellie shrugged, unable to think of an answer to the tree's question. The tree lifted Edison up out of the water again. The young boy painfully coughed up what must have been a gallon of water from his lungs. "Now listen here young-"

"Ahhhhhhhhhhhhhh – GLUB!"

It only took four words for Edison to start screaming again, and for the tree to dunk him again. GLUUUUBBBBB. "Oh dear, this could go on all night," said the tall, thin tree. It scratched one of its branches against the bark of its upper truck. "Ah, I got it."

GASP! Edison came up out of the water, heaving and coughing. He was standing waist deep in water, thirty yards from the shore. He looked around and only saw Ellie. She calmly

21

smiled and waved. He whipped his head around several times, but found no trace of the attacking tree. "Wha- . . . where . . . tree . . . attack- . . . huh?" Edison spoke in gasps.

"Ok, Ed . . . here's the deal. I think the talking tree's kind of getting a little freaked out by your screaming. So we're gonna need you to shut it. Alright?" Edison looked around the beach and then at Ellie. She made a zipping motion across her lips and motioned for Edison to respond. He nodded and shut his mouth.

"Finally!" The tall thin tree sprang up out of the water behind Ellie, and hoisted both Edison and Ellie high up into the air. With a child under each arm, the talking tree walked toward the shore. As Edison opened his mouth to scream, Ellie reached over and muffled it with her hands. Edison's frantic eyes caught Ellie's, and like the disapproving glare given to a three-year-old child reaching for the cookie jar, they silenced him.

The tree rambled on as they crossed the shore and entered the jungle. "This is unbelievable, first the vine rebellion, and now these young carbonites falling from the sky. This is truly proving to be a Council like no other. Oh, they cannot get here fast enough, where are those ice giants?" Ellie's eye popped at the mention of the Ice Giants.

"Excuse me, did you just mention the, ah . . . Ice Giants," said Ellie.

"Yes, that is who we are waiting for. You and the other carbonites will not be able to leave this island until the ice giants arrive," the tall, thin tree stopped talking and addressed Ellie. "The vines will choke every last breath from your being, and the only ones able to stop them are the ice giants."

"Uh oh," Edison made the connection.

"The uh, ice giants . . . may be a little late," Ellie was unable to look at the tree as she spoke.

The tree stopped walking. Something that looked like eyebrows crinkled on the trunk of the tree and two giant wooden pupils eyed Edison and Ellie. "Younglings, what do you know of the ice giants arrival?"

"We ah, kind of . . . well, a little root thing"

"Root thing?" asked the tree.

"Twig actually, he said his name was Twig . . . and he ah . . . he told us to attack the ice giants, and ah . . . *gulp* . . . we did."

The tree bounced heartedly, and made a hawking sound that resembled laughter.

"Hah, young carbonites . . . YOU, attack the ice giants, even if you could–" the tree stopped laughing when it looked down and saw the grave faces of Edison and Ellie. "Oh, dear."

"I don't think they're coming," Ellie looked up at the tree, like a puppy that had just peed on the carpet. Ellie braced herself for the reprimand she was sure the tree would give, but it never happened. Just as the tree was about to set Edison and Ellie down on the ground it tensed up, its branches rigid as stone. The sudden change was fluid and natural, like a hunting dog that had just heard a rabbit step on a dry autumn leaf.

As the jungle turned silent, Edison and Ellie held their breath. The sudden change in the tree's demeanor frightened them. The three peered deep into the dense jungle surrounding them. There was nothing to see. The talking tree was the first to hear it. Ellie and Edison reached out with their senses, but heard and saw nothing. Then Edison heard a very faint hum, but dismissed it for the distant roar of the waterfalls. Ellie was much more observant. She heard the hum too, but realized that just moments ago, it was not there. This was a new hum, heavier and much closer than the rumble of the falls. She also noticed that it was growing louder. She looked up at the leaves of the talking tree that held her . . . they were shaking.

"They've found us." The tall, thin tree squeezed Ellie and Edison tight, and darted off into the jungle at a full sprint. It was apparent that the talking tree was not so much running for its life, but rather, it was running for *their* lives.

6. MUD

"Who?" The tree either pretended not to hear Ellie, or chose not to answer her. Gripping Ellie and Edison tight to its trunk, the tree weaved and twisted through the dense jungle. Running in a frantic manner, as if to shake or disorient a would-be pursuer. "Who?!?!" she asked again. Apparently, now was not the best time for a conversation, but Ellie found it hard to resist. "Who's found us?"

"The Vines. The Vines have found us," the tree yelled as it ran. It was like riding a racehorse. A racehorse with twelve-foot long legs that was able to bound up, over, around, under, and sometimes even through every twist and turn in the jungle. Behind them, trees were thrown and toppled as the vines crashed through the jungle in pursuit. The vines moved like an army of ants. As one got stuck or hung up, the next in line would lunge past, often trampling those who could not keep pace. It twisted through the jungle foliage like a snake, and moved with the fury and force of a rampaging beast. Edison and Ellie didn't notice that the ground was shaking as they flew through the air. They were amazed that the tall tree seemed to be as nimble as a spider monkey, and just as quick. And as if the sight of the vines was not terrifying enough, its gargled growl, thick with saliva, sent shivers down Edison's spine.

It was once hard to see the vines through the large damp leaves of the jungle, but with each passing footstep, they drew closer. Ellie would have thought it impossible for any creature to keep up with the tree's pace had she not watched the vines do so. She never got a good look at the vines, for the tall tree zigzagged like a gazelle trying to outrun a cheetah. Just as the rushing vines came into view, the tall tree would dart around another edge of the jungle. But with every glimpse Ellie took, the vines drew closer and closer.

The tree darted over a boulder. The vines followed. As the tree jumped over a clump of thorn bushes, it caught one of its branches. It hit the ground and rolled through the mud. As it tumbled, the tree wrapped its branches around Edison and Ellie and covered them like a cage. After a half dozen rotations, they rolled to a halt in a large puddle of mud. Edison and Ellie looked up. They saw what looked like the underside of a huge, dark hammer, which just so happened to be rushing down toward them. The tree tightened its branches and rolled. SPLAT. The hammering tangle of vines missed them by inches, and sunk deep into the mud. While the soggy earth only delayed the vines attack by a few seconds, that was all the talking tree needed to be up on its feet and running once again.

After all they had been through, Edison realized that this was the first time he had heard Ellie scream. The tall tree twisted around a large outcropping of rocks, then rolled and hid behind the ruins of a large stone wall. The growl of the vines immediately silenced once it had lost sight of its prey. The snaking tangle of vines froze, rose up, and looked through the jungle for some sign of the fleeing tree and children. The talking tree pulled Ellie and Edison closer, and cradled its branches around them like a cocoon. THUMP. The vines slammed down like a hammer on a bush. An aftershock of wind rushed through the jungle and blew the hair back from Edison's forehead. He inhaled to scream as both Ellie and the talking tree covered his mouth with hands and branches. The talking tree shot Edison a "don't you dare" glare. HISSSSSS.

The snaking vines lifted their sledgehammer shaped head and inspected the flattened bush beneath it. With a low rumbling growl, the vine snake lowered its serpentine head and sniffed the broken shrub, nudging it roughly with its snout. GROWWWWLLLLLLL. There was no sign of the interfering tree or the two human children. The vine snake once again turned its attention back to the jungle. It lowered itself to the ground as the tangle of vines making up the snake's body unwound and spread out across the jungle floor. The vines covered the ground like a thin blanket, and spread out like a search party. It sounded like ten thousand wet snakes slithering in, around, and overtop of each other.

The talking tree peered out around the edge of the wall. The vines were getting closer. In less than a minute they would find the ruins of the stone wall, and then . . . find them. It had to think of something. Perhaps if it could lift the children-. Ellie shuddered, and her leg involuntarily kicked. The vines sprang to attention. The tall tree rolled its eyes, *so much for that plan.*

Edison and Ellie froze. No one dared make a sound. The vines strained to hear. Edison and Ellie held their breath, fearing the sound of a single heartbeat would expose them. It was a silent standoff. They were engaged in a deadly staring contest, and the first to blink would meet a gruesome fate. Edison was the first to see it. *Uh oh!* Ellie's small black sandal swung back and forth on her big toe. The sandal was ready to drop and fall in the large puddle beneath it on the jungle floor. Edison gestured frantically with his eyes in the direction of the teetering sandal. Ellie got the message and turned to look, just as her sandal slipped off her big toe and dropped. They were paralyzed. All they could do was watch as the sandal fell toward the puddle. And just as the small, size six, black sandal was about to hit the surface, a thin branch reached out and hooked it. Edison let out a big sigh of relief. "Wooooo!" The tall tree turned and looked at Edison in disbelief. *Have you gone mad!?!?* The slithering sound immediately stopped, and the jungle went silent. Edison gulped, "Sorry." And then the stone wall above them exploded.

The vines rushed through the wall like a freight train. Fortunately for their prey, the vines were overeager and sped past their target. Edison, Ellie, and the tall tree hugged the ground as the vines flew overhead. The vines turned and swung back. The tall tree sensed its opportunity, gathered up Ellie and Edison, and leapt for the jungle. It only took a second for the vines to wrap themselves around the tree's lower branches. Ever since Edison learned, in his third grade science class, that life on Earth was categorized as either plant or animal, he figured trees must feel some sort of pain when they are cut down. But he had never heard one scream . . . until now. The tree's scream was deep and hollow, and seemed to bounce off every tree in the jungle. As the tall tree moved to run, the vines ripped several of its branches off. The tree howled and twisted. Despite the vine snake's size and strength, the tree refused to give up. The tree lifted Edison and Ellie out of the reach of the clawing vines. The vine snake wrapped itself around several of the talking tree's branches and pulled. CRACK. CRACK. CRACK. A handful of branches broke free and sent the vine snake toppling backwards. The removal of its branches gave the talking tree just enough space to break free. Once again, it darted off into the jungle, but at a noticeably slower pace. The vine snake spat out the broken branches and took off after its wounded prey.

Ellie closed her eyes and tightly hugged the talking tree's trunk as it zigzagged through the jungle. The tree had barely enough branches to run, let alone hold on to Ellie and Edison. Edison shared Ellie's helplessness and dread. All they could do was hold tight to the tree, as the vine snake closed in on them. Edison wanted to do something to help, but what? That thought passed through Edison's mind just as the tall tree passed through a small stream. SPLASH. SPLASH. SPLASH. The depth of the water slowed the tree slightly as it had to lift its trunk legs high to get through the water. The vine snake leapt into the air like a missile heading straight for them. Edison gritted his teeth, clenched his brow, and reached out with his mind.

The water of the stream rose up and formed a clear liquid wall in front of the charging vine snake. Unfortunately, it was a wall of *water*, so with hardly any effort at all, the vines burst through. But it was enough of a distraction to ruin the vine snakes aim. So when the angry tangle of vines splashed down into the stream, it was off to the side of them and not on top of them. The talking tree paused for a brief moment to ponder the sudden wall of water that appeared, as it crossed the stream. The tree's run slowed to a walk as its roots sunk into the mud of the streambed. The vines reached out and swiped at the tree. The tree dipped under the water to dodge the strike. Ellie coughed up a lung full of water as the tree burst to the surface and ran for the jungle. The vines recoiled and lashed out again. This time the vines reached for Edison and Ellie instead of the tree. The tall tree was able to swing its branches out far enough to keep the children out of the vines' reach. The vines recoiled again. Even if the tree could get back into the jungle, it would never out run the vine snake. It had to do something, or the vine snake would rip it and the children to pieces. *Well,* thought the tree, *if it's the children it wants . . . then it's the children it will get.* It was the only way the tree would be able to save itself. The tall tree shifted Edison to a free branch, swung back, and threw him right at the vines.

"No!" Ellie screamed as Edison landed in the water right in front of the vines. Ellie clawed to free herself, but the tall tree held her tight. The vines seemed to be as surprised as Edison, and it took a moment for both to comprehend the situation. Seizing the opportunity before them, the Vines ignored Ellie and the talking tree and focused all of their attention on the Edison. Edison looked down at his mud-covered legs, and then slowly up at the tangle of vines hovering overhead. He had only one thought as the vines above him formed into a club. *Why? After all that, why did the talking tree give up and throw me to the vines?* The vine club slammed down to smash Edison.

Small stones, mud, and water flew everywhere as the vine club drove itself down into the streambed. The vines struck with such force that the level of the water momentarily lowered. As the vine snake lifted its dripping wet hammer of destruction, one of Edison's sneakers floated up to the surface. BLUB. The vine snake took a moment to savor its handy work and emitted what sounded like a satisfied, evil chuckle. The talking tree and Ellie were nowhere to be seen. During Edison's last splash, they must have run back into the jungle. CLAP. CLAP. CLAP. The vines turned to face the sound of the clapping hands coming from the jungle. Twig, the evil little root man, stepped out from behind a tree, a nasty grin stretched from ear to ear. "Nice, very nice. Now let's finish off that little girl too." Twig jumped up into the air as the vine snake twisted underneath him. With a kick of his heels and a piercing, "Giddy up!" he rode away on the back of the vine snake.

"That was awesome!" Ellie whispered.

"Thank you," the talking tree replied with what looked like a very satisfied grin. What the vine snake had not seen, was the tall tree throwing Ellie up into the jungle, and then sliding down under the surface of the water. As the vine snake slammed down on Edison, the tall tree pulled him down stream. Hidden by the fury and spray of the water, the tree was able to sneak Edison out of the water and up into the canopy of the jungle.

Ellie, hidden in the upper branches of the jungle trees, watched as Twig rode off. Perched next to her was the talking tree, and hanging upside down from one of the talking tree's branches was Edison. There was a branch wrapped around his

29

ankle, and several wrapped around his mouth to keep him quiet. The tall tree waited several minutes after the slithering of the vines had faded off into the forest, before unwrapping the branches covering Edison's mouth.

"Can I get my shoe back?"

The talking tree rolled its eyes and dropped Edison down into the stream.

SPLASH!

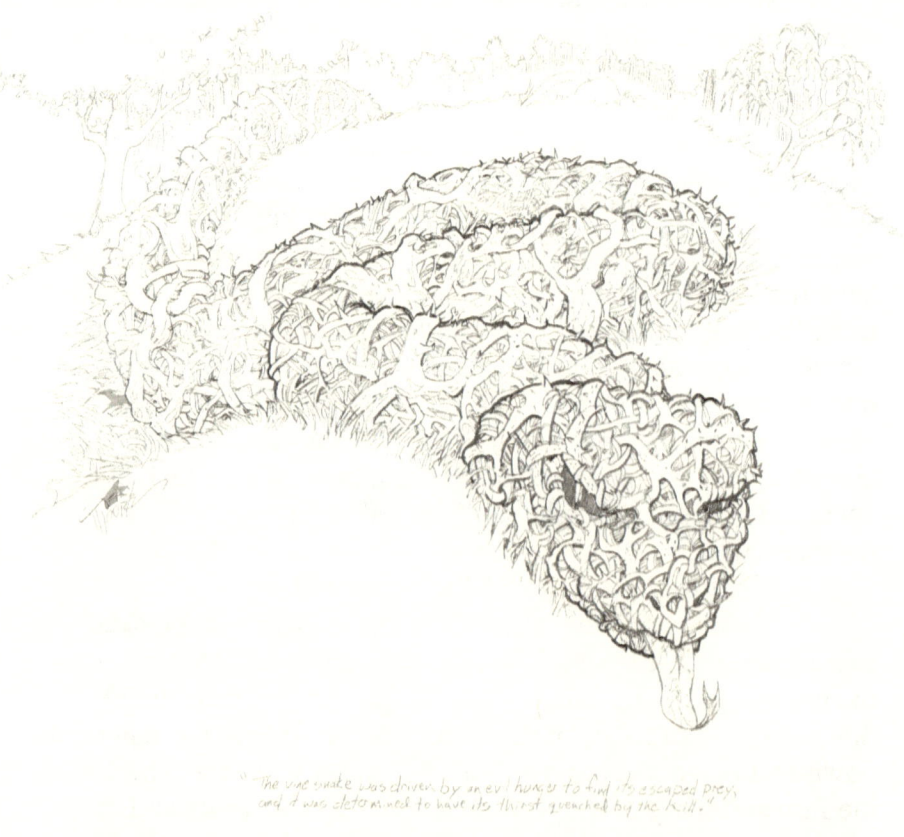

"The vine snake was driven by an evil honour to find its escaped prey, and it was determined to have its thirst quenched by the kill."

7. DEMOCRACY

After Edison retrieved his sneaker, the talking tree whisked the children away. The wind flew through their hair as they were thrown from branch to branch, high above the treetops of the jungle. With the help of the other trees in the jungle, they traveled across the submerged island. The talking tree's flight through the trees was a thing of beauty. It moved with the grace and skill of a ballerina. It even hummed something of a lullaby as it moved. Edison and Ellie felt like they had been sucked into the pages of a fairytale, as the beauty of the submerged island stretched out below them. Ellie pointed out the ruins of an old castle as they flew. Occasionally their shoulders would bump and more than once, their hands touched. After one such touch, Edison looked shyly at Ellie as if to say he was sorry. She smiled and grabbed his hand in hers.

On the other side of the island they were lowered to the ground and escorted into a dense section of trees. "Does it hurt?" Ellie leaned in and eyed the bare sections along the talking tree's trunk where its branches had been torn away.

"Quite a bit, but please . . . pay it no mind. Nothing some sunshine and a few decades of rest can't cure," said the talking tree. Edison and Ellie sat within a large, tightly packed, ring of trees. Several varieties of fruit sat before them on large green leaves. Ellie gingerly picked at the fruit as Edison gobbled it down. A steady stream of fruit juice ran from the corner of his mouth. As the talking tree dabbed bits of mud on its wounds, the ring of trees seemed to cringe and moan. The sky above them shone with the orange glow of dusk, which would soon give way to a glowing field of stars. The tall, thin tree straightened and addressed Edison. "So young one, I must thank you for your help back there at the stream. An impressive wall of water, if ever I've seen one."

"Oh, don't mention it . . . and nice move by the way. You really had me. I thought I was a goner when you threw me at the vines. WHAM! Did you see that vine hammer? Wow, I would have been smashed like a grape!" Edison lifted up a grape and

31

popped it into his mouth. "How did you know that you'd be able to pull me out in time?"

"I didn't," the tree replied.

Edison gulped.

The talking tree carefully looked Edison over. He was too busying stuffing his mouth with fruit to notice, but Ellie did, and she looked away. "Please, I was happy to help. If you don't mind, may I ask how a young carbonite such as yourself was able to perform such a task?" asked the talking tree.

"Sure, I've got super powers and I," Edison waved his hand like a symphony conductor, "can control water." Obviously, he was much more relaxed in the safety of the tree fort and with a belly full of food.

"Really?" asked the talking tree, eyeing Edison with curiosity. "Super powers?"

"Oh yeah, very super. I can make walls of water, burp bubbles, and even water torpedoes." Edison leaned back, swallowed hard and forced a belch. "Burp!" Ellie winced and waved at the air in front of her nose. Edison shrugged, "Huh . . . I guess I need to be underwater for those?"

"Burp bubbles?" asked the talking tree.

"Oh yeah. Ellie . . . hey Ellie, tell him about the burp bubble!" Ellie turned away in an apparent effort to avoid the conversation. It did not escape the talking tree's attention.

"Yes, Ellie . . . please, tell us about the burp bubbles."

Ellie could feel the weight of their stares, and sheepishly turned to face them. "Yeah, I ah . . . I've been meaning to tell you about that," said Ellie. She turned her attention to Edison as she spoke, "Do you remember when the giant wave hit our boat? I think you ran to the back after you threw up on Vivian, which was totally awesome by the way. I mean you covered her." Edison nodded. Of course he remembered throwing up on the most beautiful girl he had ever seen. A golden moment in what had been to this point, quite a stellar life. Barfing on Vivian, running to the back of the boat, barfing some more, and then looking up and seeing the huge wave . . . it was the last thing Edison remembered before waking up in the catapult.

Ellie continued, "Well, the wave actually rolled the boat over, and most of the people fell over board. My guess is that the wave was caused by whatever trench opened up around this island?" Ellie looked at the talking tree for confirmation. The tree nodded in agreement, which made Ellie feel quite pleased with herself. "So, we all fell into the water, and I think it was my dad that pulled me back onboard? Anyway, believe it or not, just about everybody got back on." Ellie's tone softened as she lowered her head. "Everyone but my grandma . . . and you. By the way, my name is Elouise, but you can call me Ellie. I don't think I'm really old enough to be called Elouise. And this is Edison." She looked up at the talking tree and thumbed over toward Edison. He nodded, as did the talking tree as they exchanged their long over due introductions.

"Pleased to meet you. You may call me Lonshallvivunstox," said the tree as he bowed.

"Lon-sha-what's-it?" Edison stumbled over his own words.

"May we call you Lyvx?" asked Ellie.

"You may, and if you would, please continue your tale."

"Oh yes, sorry . . . where was I?"

"I was drowning," added Edison.

"Uh, yeah . . . pretty much."

"See, I knew it . . . I bet no one even notic–"

"Ah hem," the talking tree politely cut Edison off and urged Ellie to continue her story.

"We looked around the boat and the water, but we couldn't find my grandmother. Edison was the last one they pulled out. You looked pretty bad, too. But you were still breathing, so the Captain just kind of stuck you in the corner. To keep you out of the way, I think? The boat's engine was flooded and just about everything electrical was shot. So, we just drifted around for a bit. Then all of the grownups started yelling at each other. And just when I thought it couldn't get any worse, the boat went over the falls."

Lyvx shuddered as he imagined a boat full of people going over the falls. "Oh, it wasn't that bad," Ellie explained. "The falls weren't that high yet, so no one really fell out. Well, except Edison . . . he fell out again. I don't think anyone was really watching you . . . sorry."

"Thanks." Edison sighed, not really feeling much love at the moment. Ellie continued her tale.

"As the water around the island drained, the boat got stuck on some trees. We all climbed down and the Captain tried carrying you down. But I think you were too heavy, or he slipped . . . and uh . . . he dropped you."

The talking tree winced.

"And it wasn't a small drop. He dropped you like twenty feet."

Edison threw his right hand up in a "why not" gesture.

"You landed pretty hard, so I went over and checked to make sure you didn't break anything. And THAT'S WHEN I noticed how white you looked. With all the barfing you were doing, you were like completely dehydrated. You were pretty out of it, mumbling and begging for water. I tried to get one of the adults to take a look at you, but they were all busy yelling at each other again. And then I tried to ask my sister Viv, but I think she was busy sunning herself. So I went and got you some water."

"Thanks."

"You're welcome. There weren't really any cups around so I had to use one of the big white buckets."

"The bait buckets?"

"Ah, are they the ones with the red and brown stains all over them?" Edison heaved and threw up a little in his mouth. "Then yes . . . sorry." Lyvx patted Edison on the back as he swallowed his own vomit. "I didn't want to wander too far, and I wasn't sure where the shore was-"

"Please tell me you didn't pee in it," pleaded Edison.

"Ouu, ack! Heck no. There was a puddle near by, so I filled the bucket there."

"Oh, thank God."

"Well . . . there was something weird about it."

"Oh no," said Lyvx as he brought a branch up to his face.

"Oh no . . . OH NO what?" asked Edison.

"Well, the water in the puddle was kind of glowing."

"Glowing, like how glowing?"

"Like really bright blue glowing."

"Glowing! . . . like toxic waste glowing?"

"Well, no . . . not really."

34

"The Veserals," said Lyvx.

"The what?"

"My sister told me it looked like blue radiator coolant, but I smelled it and it seemed OK. So I filled up one of the buckets and gave it to you." The thought of drinking out of one of the BAIT BUCKETS caused him to shutter all over.

"How much did he drink?" the tree asked.

"Well," Ellie squirmed a bit and made a face. "He seemed really thirsty, and he kept begging for more . . . "

"Oh no," Lyvx sat back and shook his trunk.

"How much?" asked Edison, as his face turned green.

"Uh, one . . . maybe two buckets."

"You gave me two buckets of glowing, blue toxic bait water?"

"It smelled fine! And look, I was the only one trying to help you, and you kept begging for more. AND I might add, you weren't very nice about it!"

"How much did he drink?" asked Lyvx.

"Uh . . . two, three . . . three and a half . . . gallons," Ellie mumbled the second part to herself, "give or take a few half gallons."

"Oh dear," Lyvx sat back and looked at Edison. "And now you have the ability to control water?" Edison nodded, like a half-naked patient in a hospital gown, apprehensively waiting for the doctor's prognosis. "Well, that would explain that."

"What explains what?"

"Hmmm, let me think . . . how best to explain this." Lyvx sat back and silently pondered Edison's question. Edison looked over at Ellie. She looked at him for a moment, and then turned away. He could tell that she felt awful, and he was much more angry with himself for how he reacted than he was at her. Not to mentioned a bit embarrassed and ashamed. After all, she was the only one who tried to help him. Heck, it was probably the nicest thing anyone had done for him in the last three years.

"I believe the Veserals, sensing your distressed state, have bonded with you," said Lyvx.

"What's a Veseral?" Edison and Ellie asked in unison.

"What's a Veseral? You don't know what a Veseral is?" Lyvx sat back, aghast and in a state of disbelief. "Huh, how you carbonites ever achieved flight is beyond me." Lyvx shook his trunk and then made a sound that Edison thought might have been a sigh. A branch came down out of the ring of trees and tapped Lyvx on the upper part of his trunk. He turned, looked up, and spoke to the trees in the surrounding ring. It was a language like none that Edison or Ellie had ever heard before. Not even in a movie or on TV. It sounded like large branches creaking and bending in the wind, and it carried on for several minutes.

Edison took advantage of the distraction and mouthed the words, "thank you" to Ellie. She blushed, and nodded back. Edison quickly and shyly looked away. The trees stopped talking and Lyvx turned back toward the children.

"It seems," Lyvx chose his words carefully, "we find ourselves in a challenging position. With the rise of the morrow's sun, the Earth's Council shall begin."

"Council, what cou-"

Lyvx cut Edison off mid-sentence. "Patience young one, your situation is not one to be rushed. The Earth Council happens every one thousand revolutions of the season."

"He means, once every thousand years," Ellie leaned in and whispered to Edison.

"I know what he means, shush!"

Lyvx eyed them both, and waited for their silence before continuing. "The Council is a meeting of the planet's essence; the Waters, salt and fresh; the Ice Giants of the North, which you are some what acquainted with . . . ; the Plants; the Vines; the Soils; and the Clays. And this year we vote."

"Vote, vote on what?" asked Ellie.

"Hrrrr," Lyvx seemed somewhat reluctant to answer. "The vote . . . this time . . . will be to decide the fate of your race." Ellie and Edison's jaws dropped. "It's been roughly twenty thousand years since a vote such as this."

"The Ice Age?" asked Ellie.

Lyvx nodded sadly..

"Well, how are we looking this time around?" asked Edison.

"Without the Ice Giants . . . not good."

8.   EARTH 101

A few years ago, Australian astronomers estimated that there were 10 times as many stars in the universe, as there were grains of sand on all the world's beaches and deserts, that's 70,000 million million million, or 70 sextillion if you prefer. Ellie thought it ironic that tonight, on what could possibly be the eve of the human race's extinction, they all seemed to be on display in the night sky. Ellie lived in the suburbs of a city ripe with car exhaust, industrial smog, and countless furnace emissions. Hence, she had never seen the beauty of a velvet night, speckled with millions of twinkling diamonds. Lyvx talked late into the night and early into the morning. Ellie wondered if the tree was nocturnal, or perhaps didn't sleep at all. She made a mental note to ask Lyvx when and if he ever stopped talking.

First Lyvx talked about the Veserals, which he found very difficult to explain. The closest comparison he could make for Edison and Ellie to understand, was that they were like microscopic bacteria. He then explained how the Veserals presided in the three original essences of the planet.

SOIL . PLANT . WATER

Lyvx then went on and on about how the number of mammals, insects, and amphibians doubled, tripled, and then quadrupled, . . . and of how they then quit counting. The increasing numbers of the Earth's inhabitants led to the formation of 'The Council.' The original numbers were set firmly at three, or so they had thought. Some felt that the cataloging of the planet's essence into only three categories was a bit general. From there, the thoughts of fairness turned to feelings of neglect, and bitterness. There had never been wars, but there were often debates, treaties, and bargaining. Alliances were formed, broken, and then formed anew.

When the Vines succeeded from the Plants, the Ice Giants were formed, in an effort to keep the numbers of The Council odd. This was done to prevent any vote that may end in a tie.

SOIL . PLANT . VINE . WATER . ICE GIANTS

Then, when the Clays sought independence from the Soils, the Fresh and Salt Waters were also encouraged to separate, in yet another effort to keep the numbers of The Council odd. And even though the flowers often rumble on about their own importance, seeding this and pollinating that, The Council numbers are quite comfortably set at seven . . . for now.

SOIL . CLAY . PLANT . VINE . FRESH WATER . SALT WATER . ICE GIANTS

Edison did his best to listen, but often got distracted by the fact that he was listening to a talking tree. Thus, when he did tune back into Lyvx's tale, it was like joining two strangers in mid-conversation. So after several minutes, he nodded off to sleep despite several forceful nudges from Ellie. Her reasons for wanting Edison to stay awake were twofold. One, she really wanted someone to discuss every single word of Lyvx's spellbinding tale with, and two, Edison snored and slept with his mouth wide open. So anytime Lyvx paused to ponder the best way to explain his tale in human speak, Ellie would ram an elbow into Edison's ribs.

"Wha . . . huh . . . I wasn't sleeping . . . zzzzzzzz." After Ellie's thirty-seventh jab, Edison woke just enough to hear her ask a question.

"How have you been able to live on the same planet with almost seven billion humans and have never been noticed?" asked Ellie.

"Hmmmm, now that is something of great relevance. In fact, I was about to bring it up myself," said Lyvx. "For we find ourselves at such an impasse this very moment. Those who have . . . stumbled upon our existence, must be judged. And if they are found to be worthy keepers of this secret, they are free to live their lives. Often times we remain in contact with each other, and mutually beneficial relationships are formed."

"How many are there?"

Lyvx frowned, "Three or four . . . I think?"

"Boy, this just keeps getting better and bet-OW," Ellie cut Edison off with another elbow jab to his rib cage.

"And what happens to those you deem unworthy?" asked Ellie

"Oh . . . well they um . . . they kind of join us."

"They join you?"

"Yes, as ah . . . a fertilizer of sorts."

"Fertilizer! You kill them!" Ellie shouted.

Edison blinked. He hoped he had nodded off, and imagined the last part about people being turned into fertilizer. Then he looked over at the expression on Ellie's face. *Darn.*

"You just kill them!" Ellie was up on her feet with arms out stretched. "Where's the boat? Where's my family!?!?"

"I hate that boat. You can turn that into fertilizer."

"Edison, shut up! Lyvx where's the boat?"

"There is no need to worry young one. The boat, and all of its occupants are safe, unconscious, but safe."

"Unconscious? What do you mean unconscious? And what are you going to do with us?" Ellie crossed her arms, wanting to make it clear that she meant business.

"So many questions young one . . . you," Lyvx scratched what looked like a jaw, and pointed to Ellie, "you will be judged. And I feel, you will be found to be quite an honorable young carbonite, and a very trustworthy secret keeper." Lyvx gave Ellie a warm pat on the head. She couldn't help but smile, but only a bit. Lyvx then turned to Edison and frowned. "Him on the other hand . . . this whole water business must–" Lyvx stopped mid-sentence and froze.

Edison and Ellie exchanged worried glances as they sat under the motionless tree. Lyvx looked as if he were listening to some distance sound, and strain as they might, it was a sound neither child could hear. This made it that much worse, because they could tell by Lyvx's reaction that whatever the sound was . . . it was not good.

After a handful of minutes, Lyvx returned from his trance. "I'm sorry children," he said, "I am needed elsewhere. Please, no matter what you do, DO NOT leave this sanctuary." With that, the talking tree rose up, and walked off into the jungle.

"What's a sanctuary?" ask Edison.

9.   FERTILIZER

"Shush . . . did you hear that?" Edison asked.

"Hear what?" said Ellie.

"I don't know. I thought I heard something."

Ever since Lyvx had left, the night got a little darker and much colder. It was as if Edison and Ellie had blinked and woken from a dream. Oz had disappeared into a puff of smoke, and they were once again alone in the real world. Marooned on a strange island where only crazy people talked to trees.

Despite their fortified cell, the children huddled together. While the ring of trees surrounding them hid the jungle from their view, it also seemed to enhance the thousands of sounds that drifted through them. What could have easily been a branch falling to the ground, may have also been a footstep. Every rustle of a leaf and creak of a branch held some sort of hidden menace. Edison was surprised to see that Ellie was every bit as jumpy as he was. It now felt as if Lyvx had not only left them, but he had abandoned them. Perhaps he didn't have the stomach to do what needed to be done, and decided to leave them to the vines? For just beyond their ring of trees, in the darkness of the jungle, the great beast stalked them. The vine snake was driven by an evil hunger to find its escaped prey, and it was determined to have its thirst quenched by the kill.

Hauntingly in the distance, Ellie and Edison could hear what they thought must be the slithering of the vines, as they move in between the trees. Occasionally, the sound drifted off only to grow louder once again in another part of the jungle. Edison couldn't decide which was more terrifying, that the vine snake was out there or that it patiently waited. Neither Ellie nor Edison spoke. Fearing that a single word might reveal their hiding place. Lyvx did tell them to stay there, but he never mentioned if he would return? *If he did abandon us, perhaps this ring of trees isn't as safe as we thought.* Ellie shook the thought from her mind. She was thinking too much, and her imagination was getting the better of her. With each new sound from the jungle, her thoughts twisted into fear and paranoia. At some point during the night, Ellie and Edison's nerves wore thin and exhaustion won over. They drifted off into the darkness of sleep.

41

When Ellie opened her eyes, things were hazy . . . and a little orange. And there was a sound . . . a scream. *Edison must have seen a bug and started screaming . . . again.* As her thoughts cleared, so did her vision. She looked up past the tops of the trees in the ring around them. The stars were gone, and the gray mist of the morning was giving way to the warm glow of dawn. She had been asleep for hours.

"Eeeeeeeeeiiiiiii!"

Ellie frowned and rolled over. She blinked. Her nose was one inch away from Edison's wide-open mouth. *Ugh!* Not only was he a snoring mouth breather, he was also fast asleep next to her. *So if he wasn't the one who screamed then who–* Ellie's thought was cut off by another scream.

"Ugh, my shoes! This will never come out! I hate this stupid, stupid jungle!!!!"

It was definitely not Edison, and . . . it was a girl screaming. A girl two years older than Ellie to be exact. Ellie recognized the voice and sat up. "Edison, wake up!" Edison snorted and rolled over. Clearly he was not a morning person. Ellie punched him in the arm, jumped to her feet, and slid out of the ring of trees.

"Ow . . . *snort*", Edison yawned, rubbed his arm, rolled over, and went back to sleep.

Ellie ran through the jungle toward the sound of the scream. The trees were so similar that it was impossible to tell where you were and more importantly, where you were going. It reminded Ellie of the time her parents took her to Round Hill Farm to pick pumpkins. She'd gotten bored, wondered off, and got lost in a cornfield. But this time she was pretty sure- . . . THUD. "Ow!" Someone not to far away had just ran into a tree. "Freak'n grrrr. I just bought this top! Grrrrr. Stupid jungle." Ellie smiled. *Yep, this way.*

"Viv!" Ellie called out as she ran.

"Elouise? Is that you?" Viv answered her sister's call.

Ellie rounded a large tree and found her sister sitting in the dirt, staring down in horror at the dirt stain on her new pink

42

designer top. "Oh my God Ellie, look at this?" Ellie ran up to her older sister and gave her a huge hug.

"I never thought I was going to see you again."

"Huh, yeah," Viv gave her little sister a small pat on the head. "Oh well, I figured you probably needed rescuing, so I came and found you."

"Needed rescuing?" Ellie pulled back.

"Hey, any luck with Gram? Did you find her?" Vivian asked. Ellie frowned as she struggled to find the right words . . . she didn't need any. Viv read her little sister's expression like a flashing neon sale sign at the mall, and then Viv's face turned pale. Ellie's grandmother was the only person they were not able to find when the giant wave rolled the boat over. In all of the confusion at the beach, Viv must have thought Ellie took off to go find their grandmother. Go figure, Viv pretty much stopped listening to Ellie at just about the exact time she discovered boys. It was at age six. Ellie didn't think it was much of a coincidence.

"This is the worst vacation ever . . . my iPhone is completely ruined. And did you see my shirt . . . see, look. RUINED!" Vivian's brand new Abercrombie & Fitch top, which her mother told her not to wear, was ruined. *So much for being the envy of the other cheerleaders on the squad.* "Stupid, dumb, smelly, gross, fishing trip from–"

"AAHHHHHHHHHHH!"

Viv froze and her eyes went wide! The familiar scream didn't faze Ellie in the least. "Did you just hear that?" asked Viv.

"Yeah, that's Edison . . . he must have woken up and noticed I was gone?"

"Who?"

"The deck hand from the fishing boat."

"Oh . . . the bait boy." Viv scowled. Clearly she had not forgotten him or his barfing on her.

"AHHHHHHHHH!!!!!!!!"

"We're over here!" yelled Ellie.

Edison was about as smooth as a porcupine. As he came running around the bend, the sight of Viv's wet, tangled, and beautiful, golden hair froze him in his tracks, "Uh, ba ba." Both Ellie and Viv turned and looked at him.

"Ba ba," were the only words Edison could find. Ellie shook her head. "Ba, um . . . I make," Edison stumbled for a word and probably chose the wrong one, "puddles."

Viv wasn't impressed, "you make . . . puddles?" Edison nodded, still in awe of the beauty before him. "You pee your pants? That's great."

"Smooth," said Ellie. She spent the majority of her young life in the shade of her big sister's visibly perfect shadow, and she hasn't been alone. She's usually shoulder to shoulder with a crowd of awe struck boys. Ellie referred to it as Viv's '*Medusa Effect.*' No snakes or statues, but plenty of hair products and babbling doofuses. Ellie pitied Edison. He never knew what hit him.

"Pee my- uh, no. That's not what I meant."

"I thought you poisoned him?" asked Viv.

"Yeah, me too. Guess not." Ellie shrugged.

"Whatever," Viv turned back toward her sister without giving Edison a second thought.

"Where's mom and dad?" asked Ellie.

"At the boat, on the other side of the island. But something's wrong with them, they're all asleep. It's like they're in a coma or something. Oh, and there's some big rock hole thing opening up that looks like it's gonna suck the boat up. Well . . . down actually."

"A big rock hole thing?" asked Ellie.

"Yeah, like one of those things grandma used to use to make hamburger meat."

"You mean a meat grinder?"

"Big hole . . . meat grinder . . . whatever! It's a HOLE, with lots of sharp gears and spiky things at the bottom."

"Puddles . . . that's not what I meant." Edison's face was flush, and his cheeks were red. He was lost in his own embarrassment, replaying the moment over and over again in his head. Wishing he had said any of a 101 different things, or perhaps better yet . . . said nothing at all.

"Mom, and Dad, and THE BOAT, and all the people on board are going to fall into a giant stone meat grinder!" It took a moment for the words to sink in, and another moment for Ellie to remember what Lyvx had said . . . *Fertilizer.* Her parents and everyone on the boat were going to be chopped up, ground down, and turned into fertilizer. Her jaw dropped and she looked over at Edison, who must have realized the same thing . . . or not. He was staring at Viv, with a goofy look on his face. Behold the power of the '*Medusa Effect*,' all boys 10-20 years old were powerless before it.

"We have to go. Now!" Ellie grabbed Viv's hand, and was about to run off into the jungle when something made her stop. It was a shadow, a very large shadow, and it was creeping up behind Edison. Both girls turned and looked over at Edison.

"*Gulp!*" *They're looking at me. Why are they looking at me? Wait! Here's my chance.* "The puddles and pee thing, that's not what I meant," Edison had his head down and was fumbling with his hands. He didn't notice the huge looming shadow on the ground until it had fully covered him . . . and Viv's golden hair. He turned around and looked up. They all screamed. But, Vivian screamed the loudest.

10. PARTING

Up until this moment, the fastest Edison had ever run was after a dare. The *'lake-effect'* dumps a lot of snow on the northeastern states, and a lot of snow can get young boys into a lot of trouble. While standing at the bus stop, waiting for the school bus to arrive, a tenth grader had dared Edison to hit the street sign with a snowball. The older boy's dare was accompanied by clucking sounds and a chicken impression. Edison knew that if he took the dare, threw a snowball, and it failed to even reach the street sign, the taunting would only worsen. Like so many other times, he was about to back down. That's when the older boy took it up a notch. Along with the clucking, chicken stepping, and arm flapping, the older boy began pecking for seeds around a small group of giggling girls. Everyone started to laugh . . . at Edison's expense. Thus, determined to ebb the current flow of the situation, he bit his lip, gulped down his pride, and began molding the tightest snowball his little hands had ever packed.

The sign was on the other side of the street. If the snowball started falling apart mid-flight, it would never make it. Edison took off his gloves as he packed the snowball, hoping that the heat from his hands would help melt the snow a bit. The cold would then refreeze it and he would have an ice ball. It had worked. Edison inhaled deeply, wound up, said a silent prayer, narrowed his aim and threw. It had the height, and it had the distance. Unfortunately, it didn't have the aim. It flew just to the right of the street sign and into a parked BMW. Edison's ice ball shattered the windshield at the exact moment the luxury car's owner walked out his front door. The chase that ensued was the fastest Edison had ever run . . . until now. At the present moment, the person chasing him was not a young stockbroker, who also happened to be a former college football wide receiver. This time, the person chasing him wasn't even a person at all. It was a giant, snarling, and tangled mesh of snaking vines. And they were dark and angry vines, with sharp, menacing thorns for fangs. This was also the scariest thing Edison had ever seen.

The chase resembled that of an old farm cat's pursuit of three field mice in the upper lofts of a big red barn. Over and under this, around and through that they went. Every time it looked as if they were cornered, the vine snake would over shoot its prey, and slam into a tree or some ancient ruins, giving the kids a few more seconds to flee. Ellie was more of a "math-a-lete" than she was an athlete. And she wasn't very fast. At least not fast enough to out run the vine snake. *Why hasn't the vine snake caught us yet?* The last time it chased them Lyvx lost half his branches. And if it weren't for dumb luck, Edison and Ellie would have been smashed to bits. Something wasn't right. Viv and Edison didn't seem to notice, but Ellie noticed . . . and she had to find out what it was. Ellie stopped running, and turned back toward the vine snake. But just as it was about to snatch her up, Edison turned back and yanked her out of harms way.

"Are you crazy?"

"Something's not right!" shouted Ellie.

"Yeah, you're not running!" responded Viv.

"But–"

"Run!" Edison and Viv shouted in unison as they yanked Ellie along. It was their first shared, special little moment. Edison looked over at Viv and smiled. And then he tripped. He rolled several feet and thudded to a stop at the base of a large tree. The dark shadow was on him. Ellie skidded to a stop and turned back. Edison screamed and covered his head. Just as the thorny vine snake was about to drop like a hammer on him, it twisted to the left and darted off into the jungle. Edison seized the moment. He scrambled to his feet and ran off after Viv. As he passed Ellie, he had to pull her along. She had stopped running again, and this time it took a little more effort to get her going.

Ellie looked at Edison as she ran. *The vines had you. They should have smashed you like a grape. There is no way they could have missed. And there is no way we can be out running that thing. In gym class I've never even made it to first base without being tagged out.* And then her mind flicked a switch and turned on the light bulb in her brain. They weren't just like field mice being chased by a farm cat . . . they actually were. This was most definitely a game of cat and mouse, and the cat was playing with them. Or perhaps . . . the cat was leading them somewhere.

"STOP!"

Viv was halfway across a small clearing when she heard Ellie. Both Viv and Edison stopped and starred at Ellie. Their faces were distorted in an even blend, one part shock and one part horror. Ellie tried to explain. "It doesn't want to catch us. It must—"

Viv cut her off, "Ellie, shut it and run," and glared at her little sister.

Edison nodded and turned to Ellie. "Yeah . . . what she said."

"What? What! WHAT?!?!" Ellie's eyes almost popped out of their sockets. By siding with Vivian, Edison had clearly struck a nerve. A delicate and highly volatile nerve, and he realized it. "What SHE SAID? Are you both blind or just complete idiots!" repeated Ellie in utter disbelief. Edison frowned, reached out his arms, and made an attempt to calm her. Before he was even able to open his mouth, he found Ellie's pointer finger right between his eyes, like an eighth-grader who had just pushed the librarian three or four steps too far. "Look Ed, just because you want to get all sucky face with my sister. Doesn't make-"

"Elouise!"

"What?" Ellie turned her fiery, red face toward her sister.

"Help," Viv's tone had drastically changed. She practically whimpered her plea. Ellie's anger quickly gave way to curiosity. Vivian was standing about fifty feet from Ellie and Edison, alone in a clearing. There was no giant, evil vine snake, no signs of distress, but something about Viv did look odd. Did she look shorter? And is she shrinking? Ellie looked down at Viv's feet, but couldn't find them. In fact, she couldn't even see her ankles. The wet, sandy ground covered Viv's feet and was working its way up her calves, or perhaps . . . she was working her way down into it.

"Quicksand," said Ellie.

"Gee, ya think?"

"Don't move!" shouted Edison.

"I CAN'T move!" Viv shouted back.

"Quick, we have to find a stick or something."

"What?" Edison's life had something of a two-minute delay to it. It usually took him a few seconds, but he did eventually catch up.

"You know, something we can pull her out with."

"A stick, right. Find a stick." Edison quickly searched the surrounding area. The quicksand was now up to Viv's knees, and her hysterics were growing. Edison and Ellie searched the ground without any luck. Edison even tried to break a long branch off of a tree. Ellie watched as the branch slipped out of his hands, slapped him in the face and knocked him back on his butt. *Sigh*, Ellie looked over at Viv, the quicksand covered her waist. *Think, think, think, think, think . . . got it.* Ellie's right eyebrow cocked as an idea popped into her head. She ran over, grabbed Edison, and pulled him to the edge of the quicksand. Ellie then motioned with her hands as if she were swishing the quicksand away with a magic wand. "Swish!"

"Huh?" If Ellie was trying to give him a signal, he had no idea what it was. Ellie smacked him on the side of the head. "Ow!"

"Ellie!" the quicksand was past Viv's waist and was slowly working it's way up over her pink Abercrombie & Fitch top. As Edison turned to look at Viv, Ellie grabbed his face and twisted him back.

"Quicksand is like fifty percent water or maybe even more."

"So?"

"So WHO do we know . . . who can control water?"

"Who?" *Wait for it . . . wait for it.* "Me!" Ellie turned back toward the quicksand and motioned like she was parting the red sea. A smile crept over Edison's face. *I can control water. And I can save Vivian's life . . . her beautiful, angel soft, warm life. And she will shower me with hugs and kisses, and love me for–* "Ow!" Ellie punched him in the arm again.

"Focus!"

"Do something!" Viv was now beyond hysterics, and too afraid to move. The quicksand was now up to her armpits.

"Edison, part the quicksand," urged Ellie.

"Part the quicksand?"

"Ellie! It would be nice if you did something . . . NOW!" Viv's arms were below the surface, and the quicksand was up to her neck.

"Part the quicksand," Edison repeated to himself. Ellie vigorously nodded 'yes.' "Ok, I can do this."

"Yes you can. And please do it now." Ellie coached him as she walked him another step closer to the edge of the quicksand. Edison adjusted his stance, cleared his thoughts, braced himself, stretched out his hands, and gave something of a mental push.

"Wow." Ellie and Viv said the word in unison. The edge of the quicksand directly in front of Edison rippled a bit, and then slowly started to part. It was like an invisible snowplow was pushing its way through the quicksand toward Vivian. For a brief moment Viv's head dipped under the surface of the quicksand, and then quickly popped back up. Edison stretched out further, as the invisible plow reached Viv and pushed the quicksand to either side of her. As the quicksand pulled away, Viv found herself standing on what looked like the bottom of a dried up lake. To her right and to her left were seventeen feet tall, sloshing, wet walls of quicksand. Viv was almost speechless.

"Awesome." She looked up at Edison and smiled. He was absolutely beaming; as long as she was smiling up at him he could hold the quicksand back for days. Edison smiled back, and even though her new pink Abercrombie & Fitch top was covered in wet sand, and her hair was a dripping mess . . . he thought she looked like an angel.

"Uh Viv, you may want to get out of there," said Ellie. She was standing next to Edison, but in his mind she could have been miles away. This was the first moment in Edison's life when he did not nervously look down or away when a girl smiled at him. He stood with his chest out and his head held high. His moment in the sun had finally come; the towel boy got in the game, scored the wining point, and won his team the state championship. The next day in homeroom, when they said his name on the morning announcements, thunderous applause would ring through the halls of his school. *Oh please, someone take a picture. Please! Please! Please!* Viv carefully stepped

50

over a large tree root and looked back up at Edison. Her smile disappeared.

Ellie felt a chill race its way up her spine. She looked down at her feet as a dark, cool shadow crept over her. "No." It happened quicker than she could have believed. Out of nowhere the giant vine snake rose up, and slithered its way toward Edison. He saw a dark flash out of the corner of his eye, as the vines struck him. They hit him with all of their fury, like a speeding freight train striking an old scarecrow. Edison flew across the clearing like a rag doll, and slammed into a huge boulder. The force of the impact knocked him out cold, and his limp body fell to the ground with a THUD.

Ellie heard her sister's scream, but was afraid to turn her head. When she finally did, the sight was every bit as horrific as she might have imagined. The towering, sloshing walls of quicksand shook violently, and for one last brief moment they hung in the air. Ellie looked down at Vivian. She was reaching out for her and trying to run, but her feet were stuck in the muck. Ellie looked straight into her sister's blank eyes as three tons of quicksand came crashing down on her. A bit of wet sand splashed onto Ellie's cheek as the pool settled. Ellie trembled as the quicksand droplet mixed with the tears on her cheek.

There was a small ripple in the quicksand at the spot where Vivian should have been. A small bubble broke the surface. And as the bubble burst, Ellie could have sworn she heard the last gasps of a muffled scream. There was no sign of Vivian, no sign of the evil vine snake, and Edison lay unconscious in a crumpled mess. Ellie fell to her knees and cried . . . alone.

11.   TRANCE

Edison woke up feeling sore. He was lying next to a large rock. Underneath his head was a makeshift pillow of sorts, a pile of leaves and moss. Edison pulled himself up and stretched. The jungle was ghostly quiet. The vine snake was gone. Kneeling in the grass, next to the placid pool of quicksand, was Ellie. Alone. There was no sign of Vivian. He had failed to save her.

"You OK?" asked Ellie, without even turning to face Edison.

"Uh yeah, I think." Edison figured at some point Ellie would become a schoolteacher, because she obviously had eyes in the back of her head. She wouldn't be one of those warm endearing English or Art teachers, she would probably end up being a Social Studies or Science teacher, the kind that would have your head spinning five minutes into the lesson. He hesitated for a moment and then, like a troublemaker walking to the principal's office, he slowly walked over to where Ellie was kneeling. His anxiety grew with every step. If Ellie got angry about being called 'awkward' she was sure to rip his head off after he had failed to save Vivian.

"Nothing broken?" she asked.

"Um," Edison looked himself over, and performed a few movements with his limbs, "no, I guess not. Sore as heck though." He looked down and noticed that Ellie had not moved an inch, and it looked as if she had been seated there for hours. "I . . . I'm sorry," was all Edison could think of to say.

Ellie looked up at Edison. "Yeah . . . me too." Her eyes were red, her face was pale and tears streaked the dirt on her cheeks. She gave Edison a half-hearted smile, and then turned back toward the quicksand.

Edison finished Ellie's sentence in his head, imagining what he thought she might have really wanted to say. *Yeah, me too! Sorry I'm about to throw you into a hungry pit of quicksand. Or . . . sorry, I'm going to make you eat both of your own nasty, smelly shoes, and then wash it down with three gallons of quicksand. Or . . . sorry, I'm going into the jungle to find a log the size of a garbage truck to beat you senseless with.* To Edison's utter amazement, Ellie did not say any of those things.

In fact, everything about her said that she was honestly and truly sorry . . . for both of them. The guilt he felt gave him the courage to ask his question, "are you all right?" *Darn it, why did I just ask that. Of course she's not alright!*

Ellie took a long deep breath before answering. "No, not really." Her eyes were blank as she stared out at the quicksand. Edison's mind raced for something, anything, he could do to offer Ellie some comfort. He remembered the warmth of his third stepmother's hand gently rubbing his back as he cried. Edison lifted his hand, went to put it around Ellie, but when he noticed how bad it was shaking, he thought better of it. He lowered his hand as a new thought popped into his head.

"We can still save your parents."

Edison's words seemed to slowly wrestle Ellie free of her trance, "Yeah, I guess we'd better go." Ellie got up, dusted off her knees, and walked off into the jungle with Edison in tow.

12.　THE COUNCIL OF THE EARTH'S ESSENCES

Both Edison and Ellie daydreamed about what the Council of the Earth's Essences might look like on their trek across the jungle island. But neither was prepared for what they found. They crept up one of the island's green peaks, and hid behind a large crumbling wall, remnants of an old castle perhaps. Below them, in a large clearing, was the Council of the Earth's Essence. Six of the seven essences were arranged in a circle. They stood on what appeared to be the giant stone altar of an ancient cathedral. While it may have lacked walls and a ceiling, the architecture of the floor, several raised landings, pillars and pylons, rivaled and surpassed any work of man. The masons and laborers of Notre Dame and the Taj Mahal would have marveled at the beauty of the great chamber, had any man or woman been allowed to enter the sacred seat. In fact, Edison and Ellie believed they were the first humans to ever bare witness to the event. That is until the mediator of the council stepped forward.

The mediator wore a crimson robe, which shone like a beacon amid the gray stone and earthen hues of the Earth's essences. The mediator looked like a toddler presiding over the coronation of a Pope. And the presiding had more of a religious air about it, than one of politics. At the center of the floor was a giant golden sun, with sparkling diamond rays etched throughout the circle. The mediator stood behind a raised podium on the far side of the sun. Scattered evenly around its edges were seven raised platforms, one for each of the essences of the Council.

SOIL . CLAY . PLANT . VINE . FRESH WATER . SALT WATER . ICE GIANTS

Edison and Ellie noticed Lyvx standing among the plants and flowers. He was the tree missing half his branches, and was glaring at the platform on the opposite side of the sun, the platform of the Vines. The Vines slithered and coiled in, over, and among themselves, like a plate full of earthworms as Twig sat on the edge of the platform swinging his feet like a child waiting for the circus to start. The platforms of the Fresh and Salt Water were shaped like bowls. Each was filled with water and had a surface like glass. Ellie pointed out that the pool of water that appeared "cloudy" was most likely the essence of the salt waters. She added that the glowing water that she fed him was from the lake, so the fresh water essences were kind of the "home team" for him. Edison didn't think her joke was very funny. The Clay essences towered like a stoic stone monolith on their podium, as the Soils swirled like a funnel folding in on itself. The platform of the Ice Giants was empty.

The mediator, standing above the essences on a tall, stone podium, lifted seven large, clear jewels above its head, and threw them. The jewels floated out into the center of the golden sun.

"Cool."

"Yeah, that is pretty cool," added Ellie.

Edison and Ellie watched as the jewels swarm through the air above the center of the platform. The seven jewels positioned themselves, one in front of each platform, and six of them floated up into the air. The jewel positioned in front of the empty platform of the Ice Giants lay motionless on the ground. The other six jewels began to glow white as they rose to hovering positions in front of the essences in attendance. The Great Council of the Earth's Essences had begun.

The Vines were the first to present their case. They were assisted by the Soils. And while Edison and Ellie were unable to understand their language, it was obvious that they had built a very strong case against the human race, and apparently . . . a strong dislike as well.

A thick tangle of vines stretched out into the center of the ring, and formed what looked to be a giant picture frame. A good-sized wad of the swirling soil shot out and struck the center of the vine frame. It combined with the vines, filled the center of the frame, and formed a smooth, blank canvas. Ellie didn't have to wait long for Edison to ask what was happening.

"What's happening?"

"No idea. How about we sit here quietly behind this nice big safe wall, and watch," said Ellie.

Edison nodded, and then asked another question. "Do you think they're good guys or bad guys?"

"Well, the Vines have tried to kill us . . . twice."

"Right . . . good point, bad guys. So I guess the soils are bad guys too?"

Ellie nodded and turned back toward the council. There was movement in the vine frame. The soil canvas swirled and formed the shape of a World War II flying bomber. The frame and its images were large enough for Ellie and Edison to read the writing on the side of the plane's nose, *The Enola Gay.*" The soil canvass shifted, as the image of the plane flew through some clouds, opened its payload doors, and dropped a large bomb. The inside of the frame flashed as the soils revealed the large, menacing mushroom cloud of the atomic explosion. The image lingered long enough for everyone to see, and then it disappeared. Next the image of a large oil tanker swirled onto the soil canvas. The writing on the side of the oil tanker read, "Exxon Valdez."

"Well, kiss the human race goodbye," Ellie whispered to Edison.

"Huh?" It wasn't until Edison saw the oil covered seagulls, ruined shoreline, and black pools of spilled oil, that he made the connection. The soils swirled the image of a baby sea lion onto its canvas, and then showed the calf crying, blinded, and covered head to toe in oil. But as quickly as the tortured, oil slick gulls and oil soaked sea lion appeared, they swirled into a new shape. It was the image of an offshore oil platform, with the initials 'BP' prominent on one side. The platform shook and then exploded. Black oil bubbled up to the surface, polluting the surrounding seawater. "When did that happen?"

"Last summer," Ellie turned toward Edison. "Have you ever even seen a newspaper?"

"A what?" Ellie's eyebrows rose. "I'm kidding . . . I don't think I've ever read one though?" Ellie rolled her eyes and turned back toward the council. The soil making the image of the polluted gulf waters swirled about and formed another image, a nuclear power plant.

"Chernobyl," whispered Ellie.

"Cher what?" asked Edison.

"You'll see," Ellie pointed toward the vine frame just as it lit up. Edison wasn't sure what had happened, but figured it must have been bad. He also marveled at how Ellie knew so much about everything. For Edison, this was as painful as it was frustrating. It was like tuning into a movie halfway through and having no idea what was going on. And each time he tried to ask, Ellie shushed him. Inside the vine frame, the image of the ruined nuclear power plant swirled into the fog-covered skyline of a 1940s smog-infested steel town.

"Oh great," said Ellie.

"What, what's that?" asked Edison.

"That's where I'm from."

"Where?"

"Pittsburgh, but it doesn't look like THAT any more. In fact, it now has one of the largest concentrations of "green" buildings in the world and was even voted most livable city in . . ."

"Where's that?" The image of the old steel town transformed to a hazy, over crowded, modern day city, teaming with gridlock and automobiles.

"China . . . I think?"

The environmentally destructive glory of mankind unraveled itself inside the vine frame, and the voting members of the Earth's essences had front row seats.

13. VOTE & VERDICT

The Vines presented their case for two long hours. Both Edison and Ellie grew increasingly uneasy as they watched. Edison because his butt hurt, and Ellie because she knew it would take a miracle to successfully argue against the case presented by the Vines. All the blunders and ignorance of mankind had been carefully documented, and the Earth had the scars to prove it. When they were done, the Vines and the Soils retreated back to their platform as the Plants, and only the Plants, rose to defend the human race.

A large, green hedge calmly walked out into the center of the circle. It looked and waddled like a porcupine, with long, leafy branches instead of quills. Once it got to the center, it stopped, and shivered. Edison and Ellie held their breath. The branches on the hedge drew in close, formed a tight shell around its body, and then slowly, like a flower rising through the soil, a single branch rose into the air. It sprouted several small leafy branches that elegantly twisted into a shape.

"Wow, these things are cool," said Edison, a bit louder than he should have. Several vines twitched as if they had heard something, separated from the clump, and began twisting around. Ellie slapped a hand over Edison's mouth and yanked him back behind the wall. "Sorry," Edison said with a meek smile. Ellie glared at him. They waited several minutes before sneaking a peek at the council. When they finally did, they were relieved to see that the Vines had turned back toward the center of the circle, and were fully engrossed in the drama unfolding before them.

The branches of the hedge twisted into characters that moved and interacted like puppets. Ellie was more than a bit annoyed that Edison had caused them to miss the first part of the plant's case. What they saw now was the leafy image of a man. He had a hammer, and a chisel in his hand. He was a sculptor. And slowly the clump of bush next to him transformed into a tall man. It was the statue of David, and the sculptor was Michelangelo, one of mankind's greatest artists. The leaves on the branches shivered as if a wind were blowing through them, and then transformed into a new shape. It was the shape of a giant Egyptian pyramid, and then with a shiver it turned into the

Sphinx, the only remaining monument of the Seven Wonders of the Ancient World.

"How the heck is that going to help us?" asked Edison, in a very hushed voice.

"They're trying to present the culture, beauty, and peacefulness of humans, through great works of art and architecture . . . I think?" said Ellie. *Boy, they better have a big ending planned.*

The branches twisted into the Eiffel Tower, the Mona Lisa, the Coliseum, Machu Picchu, the Hanging Gardens of Babylon *(or at least Ellie thought they were)*, several grand cathedrals, and then finally two small hands. The hands belonged to a young schoolgirl, perhaps five or six years of age. She was planting a seed. One by one, and row by row, a field of children appeared. They were all planting seeds. The children disappeared as small sprouts broke the surface of the ground, grew into a long row of oak trees, and rose high into the air. The canopy of the mighty trees grew together like a large circus tent, and slowly transformed into a new shape. A small bundle-like-patch, held tightly in the arms of a large bundle. It was a mother holding her infant. Two more figures appeared, a smaller one and a taller one. The four green leafy figures stood tightly together, fastened by the embrace of the tallest two. It was the truest example of love mankind knew, a family.

"Well, if that's all they got . . . we're screwed!" said Edison.

"Shush!"

With a final shiver, the green, leafy family disappeared as the branches shrunk back into the porcupine hedge. Lyvx stepped down from the Plants' platform and walked over to the hedge. He spoke in a weird language, and gestured several times toward the empty platform of the Ice Giants and the floating crystals. This caused the Vines and the Soils to speak up with angry tones. Ellie wasn't sure, but she thought perhaps Lyvx was trying to postpone the vote. Lyvx and several other Plants then began to argue with the Soils and Vines. The Clays also joined in, siding with the Vines. And just as it looked like things were about to spiral out of control, a blinding white light shone from the crystals, accompanied by an ear-piercing ring. The glaring light and tone immediately silenced the squabbling essences. The ringing died out, and the glow subsided as Lyvx frowned and walked back to his platform. The small porcupine hedgehog waddled closely behind the broken tree.

An air of anticipation and tension filled the chamber. Ellie noticed that the demeanor of the red, robed mediator had also changed. While the mediator still stood tall with the authority of a court judge, a new sadness had crept in. The audience of the earth's essences was silent as the mediator raised her hand. Ellie was surprised to see the hand was somewhat boney, and distinctly feminine. She turned to the platform of the Clays. A large mound of clay gave what looked like a nod now that the mediator returned. She turned to each of the platforms, and repeated the process. Once it was complete, she lowered her hand and bowed her head. It was time to vote.

The Vines were the first to cast their lot. The white jewel floating before them turned a dark shade of red. And then as if to answer their vote, the white jewel floating in front of the Plants' platform turned bright blue. The Soils were the next to vote. Their jewel also turned dark red, no real surprise thought Ellie. It wasn't hard for her to realize that red meant bad news for the human race. The Clays voted next. Their jewel also turned dark red. The Salt Waters then voted, bright blue. And finally the Fresh Waters voted, bright blue.

RED: **Vines . Soils . Clays**
BLUE: **Plants . Fresh Waters . Salt Waters**

Three to three, the vote was tied. The Vines and Soils stirred, angered by the outcome of the vote. Edison and Ellie couldn't understand the language they spoke, but by the way they were waving about and pointing at the empty platform of the Ice Giants, it was quiet clear they wanted another vote. Ties were not something that happened in the Great Earth Council. The mediator stepped forward and quieted the crowd. As she lifted her hand the seven floating jewels turned back to their original shade of white. She then clenched her fist, and lowered her hand. Four of the seven floating jewels turned black, as if their flame had been snuffed out. The four darkened jewels fell to the ground. Three white jewels remained in the air, the number of the earth's original essences. The Vines were now more upset than before as their voting jewel was one of those that were snuffed. Ellie wasn't sure, but she thought that Lyvx, standing among the plants, was smiling. The Plants still had their voting jewel. The Soils and the Salt Waters also had their voting jewels. While the Vines were in a tizzy, the Clays and the Fresh Waters seemed quite indifferent. Ellie was delighted to see that the Salt Waters, which voted not to extinguish the human race, still had a vote. Were the essences to vote the same way, as before, it would be two to one in favor of saving mankind. But Ellie and Lyvx weren't the only ones aware of this. The Vines jumped down from their platform and began thrashing and flailing all over the floor of the council. This in turn caused Lyvx and the Plants to jump down and argue their case as well. The mediator did her best to listen to both the Plants and the Vines, but the debate quickly escalated into a chest-beating match.

"Oh, hey look . . . the Soils are getting a drink," said Edison as he pointed toward the pool of salt water. A small portion of the Soils snuck off their platform, and crept over to the Salt Waters. It looked as if they were talking.

"It's a distraction," Ellie answered.

"What's a distraction?"

"The Vines, the reason they're stirring things up so much is to distract everyone . . . well, distract everything I guess. See over there, no one's paying any attention to the Soils. They've snuck over to the Salt Waters, and are probably trying to get them to switch their vote. We have to do something. We have to tell Lyvx."

"Too late." Edison pointed down toward the council.

The seven crystals rose up, shined bright white, and rang out loudly. The Plants and Vines winced, and once again retreated back to their platforms. When Ellie looked over at the Salt Waters, there was no sign of the Soils. Whatever they had to say, or deal they had to broker, it had been done.

The mediator bowed her robed head, and took a step back as the three, clear crystals rose for the final vote. The Plants' jewel was the first to change color. It glowed a bright shade of

61

blue. Their vote was immediately followed by the bright red glow of the Soils' jewel.

"Cool, the Salt Waters will vote blue again and we're saved. Come on, let's go to the boat," said Ellie. As she stood and dusted the dirt off her legs, her entire body froze. The Salt Waters had cast their vote, and their jewel turned blood red.

RED: **Soils . Salt Water**
BLUE: **Plants**

Edison and Ellie were speechless. The Plants looked shocked as well. The Vines however, showed no surprise. It was as if they had known the outcome before it happened. Edison had no way of knowing for sure, but it looked as if the Vines were smiling.

The mediator stood silent at the edge of the great circle, as the Vines slithered into the center of the ring. They were animated as they yelled something in their language. The Plants seemed to object and they lunged off their platform, diving straight for the Vines. It was frightening to see the large trees move so quickly, and with such violent intent. Compared to the other trees, Lyvx was the size of a small child. Just as they were about to engage the Vines, the ground of the great circle shook. Giant clay and soil figures rose up from the ground and blocked the path of the charging plants, like a line of riot police in front of an angry group of protestors. The shapes of soil and clay creatures were a cross between dinosaurs and giant mammals. One particularly menacing beast was a cross between a tyrannosaur and a mountain gorilla.

A soil beast motioned toward the glowing jewels, as the plants reluctantly stopped their charge. While the plants may not have liked the outcome, they were bound by the glowing red verdict. It was the way of the Council. The smallest tree among the plants turned its trunk and ever so slightly twisted up toward the nearby hilltop. It was Lyvx, and he was staring directly at Edison and Ellie. Both of the children gasped and scrambled back behind the stone wall.

"Oh man, he knows we're here. How does he know we're here?" Edison was frantic. "What are we going to do?"

62

"I don't know," said Ellie.

"We're dead, we're all dead. They're gonna wipe out everyone. Everyone on the planet! How are they going to do that?"

"I don't know." Ellie peaked around the edge of the wall and watched as all seven crystals turned red. Even the Plants' crystal now gave way to the crimson cast of the majority, and turned red. The seven red crystals slowly turned onto their sides and floated toward the council floor. Underneath the seven crystals, seven slots in the golden floor opened. The crystals lowered themselves into the slots, and with a hollow stony CLUNK, they settled into the open notches. The glowing red light of the crystals slowly traced its way around the outline of the giant sun. The once golden sun on the floor of the council now glowed an ominous shade of red. Once the outline was complete, a second very loud CLUNK reverberated across the submerged island. It was as if the door to the center of the earth had just been unlatched. The echo drifted out across the water, and faded away into the roar of the waterfalls as the giant golden floor of the council slowly began to turn.

It was an amazing sight for the two children watching on the hill. "Cool," said Edison, as he rubbed his eyes. It had been several minutes since the last time he had blinked. Edison and Ellie watched as the circle completed a full rotation. SHUNK, a slight tremor moved across the island. *An earthquake?* Ellie leaned forward and squinted.

"It's growing," said Ellie.

"What is?"

"The circle. Watch, with each full rotation, the circumference of the circle increases." Slowly the image of the red glowing sun rotated. "Look at the edges, right . . . now!" The edge of the circle grew another three inches as a faint rumble rung in Ellie's ears and the ground beneath them shook. Ellie grabbed Edison's shoulder to steady her self.

"Did you feel that? I think the whole island just shook." Edison looked to Ellie for answers. Ellie's eyes widened as the light bulb in her brain switched on.

"No, it's not the island. It's the planet."

14. HERE, THERE, EVERYWHERE

San Jose, California, United States.

   A young woman knelt in the dirt of a flowerbed in front
of a small, white, single story house. A brown and white beagle
nosed its way under the woman's right arm and sniffed the
violets resting in the fresh soil. The woman pushed the dog
away, as the ground shook. She lost her balance and fell onto her
elbows. The beagle snuggled in tight to her owner's side and
whimpered.

Paris, France.

   A waiter smiled as he took the camera that was handed to
him. He framed a nice shot of the two middle-eastern tourists
seated at the outdoor café. He bent down to make sure the top of
the Eiffel Tower was in the picture. The older couple smiled, and
squeezed each other's hand. It had always been the woman's
dream to visit Paris. As the waiter pressed down on the button,
he lowered the camera and missed the shot. His jaw hung open.
The man and woman turned around, and looked on in disbelief.
The top of the Eiffel Tower was swaying. Its steal beams
creaked as its foundation twisted.

North Pole, Artic Circle.

   A small harp seal bounced through the surf as the large
orca snapped its jaws in pursuit. The seal raced along the edge of
a giant glacier, desperate to find a small outcropping to provide
safety from the killer whale. The seal was beginning to tire as the
jaws of the predator drew closer with every snap. Just ahead of
the seal, about five feet above the cold water was an ice ledge. A
five-foot jump from the water was nothing for a well-rested seal,
but fatigue was taking a firm grasp on its body. There was no
time for doubt. Not making the jump meant only one thing,

instead of spending the evening with its herd, it would spend it in the belly of the black and white beast. The seal doubled back over the killer whale's dorsal fin. A small stream of blood lit the water as one of the orca's teeth grazed the seal's rear left flipper. The seal dove down and under the whale, pushing the water toward the surface with all its might. The twenty-two foot killer whale struggled to turn its hulking mass, giving the seal the precious few moments it needed. The seal broke the surface and flew up toward the ledge. It twisted its backside like a high jumper in an effort to leap a few extra inches. The seal's belly hit the edge of the ice, hung in mid air for a moment and then fell backwards. She landed in the icy water with a splash. The water churned as the killer whale stretched its jaws wide and lunged for the trapped seal. Its pink tongue twittered with excitement. And just as the jaws were about to close on its dinner, SPLASH. A chunk of ice, roughly the size of a three-story office building, cracked off the glacier, slid into the water, and crushed the killer whale. The small seal popped its head out of the cold water and sniffed the air. A large crack opened along the side of the glacier. It ran over the edge and stretched out toward the northernmost tip of the planet.

15.   PASSING SENTENCE

"The what?"

"The plates! They're moving?"

"What's moving where?" Just when Edison thought he couldn't be more confused.

"The Earth's tectonic plates, they're moving. Of course they're always moving, except they're supposed to move really, really slowly, only a few centimeters per year. But I think THEY, the Council, just moved the plates three inches in a minute. Hold on." Ellie and Edison braced themselves as the council floor completed another rotation and expanded another three inches. Once more, the submerged island rumbled as it shook.

The shock Ellie felt at the outcome of the essences' vote paled in comparison to the terror she now felt at the swiftness of the judgment handed down by the Council. Unlike Edison, she was not one of those "freak out" people. When things fell apart around her she stayed calm. Her grandmother used to affectionately refer to Ellie as her little *'eye of the storm.'* All of her "freaking out" was internal, sometimes causing her to go into something of a quiet shutdown mode. As Edison all but pounded his head against the stone wall, Ellie stood frozen with her eyes transfixed on the ground before her. She was just about to enter a heavy panic trance when something interrupted her. There on the ground before her was a lone dandelion. It was bouncing up and down and . . . waving. Ellie looked over at Edison. He was too busy pulling his hair out to notice their new visitor. She looked down at the little dandelion man, who now appeared to be quite cross, with its pedals folded in a stern stance. Once the dandelion was sure it had Ellie's full attention, it ran around to the front of the stone wall and motioned toward the Great Council. Ellie followed, and gasped in horror at what she saw.

"Aw crap!" She immediately turned back, grabbed Edison by the hand and ran, pulling him down the backside of the hill.

"Where are we going?" asked Edison.

"To save the boat, and then 8 billion people!"

16.   PLAN A

The glowing, red sun on the council floor continued its rotation. Ellie and Edison reached the back side of the hill and snuck through the jungle to the rear of the council circle. They could see a new event unfolding. And this time Ellie didn't need to explain what was happening. Edison could see it quite clearly with his own eyes. The extinction of the human race was about to start . . . with his stepfather's fishing boat. A plume of black smoke rose high into the air. The fishing boat teetered back and forth, delicately balanced on the top of a tall stone pillar. Next to the boat, a crack in the earth widened. Dark smoke spilled out of the crack. The edges of the newly formed pit glowed, a result of the bubbling lava below. There were no screams as the smoke rose. Everyone on the boat was still unconscious. And there was no one to sound an alarm as the Vines, like a ghoulish hangman, stalked toward the boat. Edison imagined the Vines must have been delighted to be the ones to strike the first blow against the human race.

"So where's the big, stone meat grinder?" wondered Ellie.

Edison shrugged. "Does it matter? Giant stone meat grinder, bubbling pit of lava . . . they both suck!"

No one noticed as Ellie and Edison snuck out from the trees and crept toward the Council. They hid behind the vacant platform that should have been occupied by the Ice Giants. The small dandelion creature, now perched on Ellie's left shoulder like a pirate's parrot, led them to the spot. She estimated 50 yards of grass stood between them and the fishing boat. The Vines were now at the base of the pillar that held the boat. Thick, dark green vines crawled up the pillar, like the tentacles of a hundred giant squids. Each one more anxious then the next, racing to be the first to plunge the boat into the lava pit. Perched on the edge of the submerged island, the lava hissed as droplets of water from the falls fell into the flaming abyss.

Edison stood frozen in a trance, like a farmer watching swirling winds form into a volcano's funnel cloud. While Ellie was also in awe of the spectacle—who gets to see a giant vine snake throw a boat into a pit of lava on a daily basis—if did not stop her from accessing the situation and devising a plan. After all, staying cool, calm and collected in a time of crisis was her gift. She looked from platform to platform . . . nothing. She looked at the boat . . . nothing. She looked at the vine snake, definitely nothing. She looked at the Vine's platform and saw Twig seated on the edge, grinning from ear to ear. *Ouuu, I hate him.* Ellie blinked him out of her thoughts and looked around the Council once more. For a brief moment she thought she saw the red-cloaked mediator looking at her. *Huh?* She did a double take and found the mediator casually sneaking a look in her direction. *Was it possible the mediator knew they were here? Why was she not saying anything? Did she think they posed no threat? Was she trying to help? Was she human? And if so, how could she sit by and do nothing as the essences condemned the human race to extinction?* Twenty questions raced through Ellie's mind, and another fifty would have followed had the mediator not nodded toward the council floor.

The red glow of the rotating floor was brightest at its center. It was also the place where the mediator nodded. Evenly spaced around the heart of the red sun, were the seven crystals of the earth's essences. The dandelion man must have sensed what Ellie was thinking, because she was certain she heard him giggle. She returned his naughty giggle with a smile, and then turned to Edison. "OK, you've got to go!" and gave him a shove.

"What? Go? Go where?" asked Edison.

"That way! Sneak along behind the platform on the RIGHT SIDE, not the left. The right! And then run behind those bushes to the boat."

"Then what?"

"I don't know, do that water thing of yours and save the boat!"

"Water thing?"

"Yeah, duh . . . look the whole freak'n island is surrounded by WATER! Use it! Figure something out, alright. I'll get everyone's attention and YOU save the boat." Before Edison had a chance to ask another question, Ellie sprang to her toes, grabbed him by the shoulders, and planted a small kiss on his cheek. To say it shocked Edison would have been an understatement. He wasn't sure how he imagined his first kiss from a girl would happen, but he definitely didn't imagine it would be like this. *And for that matter, did a kiss on the cheek count?* "For luck," Ellie added with a smile as she spun away. The dandelion creature held on tight as she whirled around, and ran in the opposite direction. *A kiss is a kiss right, it had to count . . . cheek or not. Right?*

"Hey, where are you going?" Edison called out in a hushed whisper.

"This way! You go THAT way! Go save the boat, and then don't forget to come save me." Ellie turned and ran into the center of the Council.

17.   WHICH ONE?

The essences were still as they watched the Vines slowly wrap themselves around the fishing boat hull. No one objected and no one tried to stop them from tossing the boat into the lava pit. And no one seemed to care that there were twenty-three unconscious people on board. There were no ripples in the shallow pools of salt or fresh water. And there was no swaying of the tall trees on the Plant platform, until one of the smaller trees heard its named being called. The small tree tilted its top stems and twisted its trunk back toward the Council circle.

"Pssssssst. Lyvx!"

Lyvx jumped when he saw Ellie standing in the center of the Council with an armful of crystals. At her feet was the small dandelion-man, carefully teetering back and forth with a crystal twice the size of its body held above its yellow, pedaled head. Lyvx gasped in shock, as Ellie smiled and waved. The dandelion-man also waved. "Which one's the Vines? And which one is the Soils?" Lyvx was speechless. He looked down at the council floor and saw that it was no longer rotating, and that the red glow of the sun had vanished. He looked up and saw Ellie pick up another crystal. She lost her balance and one of the crystals fell from her arms. Lyvx gasped and raised a branch to his mouth. Ellie caught the falling crystal just before it hit the stone floor.

"Whoops, how about this one?" Ellie asked. She held up another crystal and waved it at Lyvx. While she had no idea what the crystals were, she could tell by Lyvx's reaction they were important. Lyvx checked to make sure no one was watching before answering.

"Child, have you gone mad? Put those down this instant!"

"No. I bet it's this one?" With the help of the dandelion-man, Ellie pulled out the final crystal. SHUNK.

"You must stop!" Lyvx whispered, not wanting to been seen or heard by the other essences.

"Hmm, let's see . . . they killed my grandmother, my sister, and now they're going to kill my parents, and oh yeah . . . you're planning on wiping out the human race. So let me think . .

71

. uh, NO!" Ellie put down the crystal in her hand and picked up another one. "This it?"

"Child, your sister she . . . NO NOT THAT ONE!" Ellie had obviously picked up the crystal that belonged to the Plants. She held it high, as if to smash it on the ground.

"Which one is the Vines?"

Lyvx frowned and pointed to the crystal that was in the arms of the dandelion-man. Ellie picked it up, with the dandelion creature still swinging on the end.

"And the Soils?"

Lyvx reluctantly pointed to a crystal that was lying on the ground next to Ellie's foot. Ellie picked it up mid-stride as she ran toward the edge of the council. She was so focused on her plan that she didn't hear Lyvx's final words, "your sister is not dead."

18.   CLANK CLANK

Twig rocked back and forth and clapped his hands, as the Vines pulled the fishing boat down off the stone pillar. They turned toward the council and presented it for all to see. There was something very ceremonious about the presentation. The Vines looked at each and every essence, making sure all could bare witness to the dreadful deed it was about to perform. They wanted to make sure that all the attention fell on them, and it did. So much so, that no one noticed the council floor had stopped rotating and no longer glowed red.

The Vines rose high, like a proud man puffing out his chest, and turned toward the lava pit. It slithered to the edge of the pit with the boat held high. And just as it was about to hurl the boat into the bubbling lava at the bottom of the chasm a sound rang out. CLANK. The Vines froze for a moment. CLANK. CLANK. And than all at once, every essence slowly turned back toward the great circle of the council. CLANK. CLANK.

Standing as tall she could, on the empty platform of the Ice Giants, was Ellie. She held two crystals, one in each hand, like drum sticks. She was poised to strike them together. Twig turned and fell from his platform in disbelief. Ellie wasn't sure, but she thought she heard the Vines make an angry hiss. The dandelion-man on Ellie's shoulder scampered around and hid behind her back. Ellie smiled and waved the crystals at the Vines. CLANK. She slammed the crystals together again. Like a wild animal acting on pure instinct, the Vines dropped the boat and charged. Fortunately, the boat landed on the edge of the pit and not inside. With a small squeal, Ellie turned and ran.

She jumped off the empty platform and ran across the Council floor just as the Vines slammed down on the opposite side of the golden circle. The Vines landed like a giant, gray back gorilla lunging out of a tree. Ellie ran toward the Plants' platform, and despite Lyvx's frantic waving and pleas, she jumped up onto it. She ran through the trees, darting between and around the tall trunks, and then out the other side of the platform. With no regard for the plants or trees, the Vines dove after Ellie. Before they were able to round the first tree trunk,

73

their progress was halted. In the form of the coiled snake, the Vines were easy to grab. And they were grabbed, by the largest tree on the platform and yanked high into air. The Vines were shocked and taken off guard, which made what happened next all the easier for the tall oak. With the might of a medieval catapult, the branches of the tall oak swung up and threw the Vines high into the air. They spun wildly, like a twisting cat in free fall trying to land on its feet. The effort was in vain as the Vines flew across the council, past the shoreline, over the shallow waters, and into the waterfall ring.

"Alright!" A young boy's voice rang out. Slowly all of the essences, and even Ellie turned. There was Edison, standing in the open with his fist raised, and a lump forming in his throat. Ellie frowned and shook her head. The dandelion-man on her shoulder buried his pedaled head into his stems. Ellie's distraction had given Edison the chance to sneak past the council platform, and cross half the distance of the field to the boat. But his sudden joyful outburst rang out like a fire alarm, and evaporated the element of surprise like a drop of water falling on the glowing, red coals of a campfire.

"Aw man," Edison's shoulders slumped as he realized his mistake, and they fell even lower when he saw Ellie's glare. She stood, hands on hips, at the back of the Plants' platform, her face as red as the crystals in her hands. The Soils were the first to act. The large earthen heap separated and divided into a dozen four-legged beast-like creatures. Both Ellie and Edison tensed, not knowing which one of them the soil beasts were about to charge.

And then with a roar, the waterfall ring surrounding the island exploded as a very angry and wet vine snake burst out. Ellie lifted her arm to shield her face, as she was pelted by the spray from the watery explosion despite the distance. The soil beasts reared back on their haunches and rang out a shrieking war cry. Then all twelve beasts turned and charged toward Edison.

"Ahhhh," Edison screamed as he ran. Not knowing what to do, he ran to the boat, jumped over the side, and dove in. He hit the deck, hid his head under his hands, and assumed the crash position. He waited for the beasts to jump over the side of the boat and pounce on him. He waited . . . and waited . . . and waited . . . and waited. Edison slowly opened his eyes. He noticed that, aside from the black lava plume, there were no clouds in the sky. Not one. Clear blue as far as the eye could see. *And you know what, I don't care what anyone says; a kiss on the cheek DOES count.* He was the type of person who got distracted easily. But reality, like it often does, quickly returned Edison to his predicament. The boat rocked and tilted sharply to the right. Edison grabbed a hold of the side rail to steady himself as the boat was lifted into the air.

"Uh oh," he peered down over the side of the boat. Yep, it was the soil beasts all right, all twelve of them. They had lifted the boat and were carrying it toward the large, bubbling, red lava pit. "Crap." He had to think of something quickly. Unfortunately, all he could think of was how he wished Ellie were here, so she could tell him what to do. *Where the heck is Ellie?*

19.   PLAN B

Ellie dove over the Soils' empty platform, just as the vine snake shot past. In its fury, the vine snake, flying recklessly at full speed, was unable to turn. It shot across the council circle, and crashed into a stone wall just outside the ring. The violent impact loosened several large stones, falling onto the vine snake. It writhed in anger as the stones crushed and trapped parts of its body.

Ellie, who was crouching under the floating stone platform, didn't wait for the vine snake to free itself. Scrambling on her knees, she turned and scurried out from the other side. Just as she was about to run toward the jungle, a thin stringy pair of hands reached down and plucked one of the crystals from her arms. It happened so quickly that it took Ellie several seconds to realize what had happened. Clutching the one crystal she still had tightly in her arms, she stood up and looked over the stone platform. A familiar face stuck its forked tongue out at her, and then ran off toward the vine snake. It was Twig, the nasty, little root man. He now had one of the red crystals, most likely the Vines' crystal, and was running off to return it to the vine snake.

"Crap!"

Ellie darted under the platform, dove forward, and reached as far as she could with her free hand. She caught Twig's leg just as he hit the ground. He went sprawling and the crystal flew from his hands. He twisted back and with a kick to Ellie's face, freed himself. He scrambled on all fours to reach the crystal, and clutched it tight with both hands. He took the briefest of moments for a small sigh of relief, which was all the time Ellie needed. She never broke stride as she got to her feet, heaved her crystal back like a baseball bat, and then swung for the fences.

She figured Twig to be made of a thousand tangled roots, which would make him very dense and heavy, but she was wrong. He was actually quite light, like a softball. Which, incidentally, was exactly how he flew. Like a well-trained base runner, Ellie didn't stop to admire her swing. She picked up the Vine's crystal, which Twig had dropped, and sprinted back toward the Council.

She ran straight for the stone podium of the mediator. "Excuse me, coming through." The mediator was almost at the bottom of the podium steps when Ellie reached it. Ellie knocked her down as she ran past and up. "Sorry." The stone podium looked to be several thousand years old, and perhaps the handy work of the ancient Mayans or Incas. It was shaped like one of those portable staircases used by hardware stores to retrieve paint cans and lumber from high shelves. To Ellie's surprise, it was much taller than it looked. In fact, from the top of the hill the council circle only looked to be fifty or sixty feet across. But now that she was on it and running for her life, she could see the council circle was at least a hundred feet across. Her legs began to tire as she ran up the tall steps of the podium. Obviously, the thousand-year-old person it was originally built for was much taller, and had longer legs.

As Ellie crested the top step, the vine snake crashed onto the bottom step. The impact shook the podium, and sent Ellie over the front edge. She cradled the two crystals in her left hand, and hung onto the platform edge with her right hand. For a brief moment it looked like the towering structure would tip, but it soon rocked back to a resting position. Ellie hung off the front of the podium, her feet dangling helplessly in the air. The podium was much taller than she had expected, and the height delivered an un-welcomed dizzying effect.

She had two choices. Fall, break both of her legs, get pounded to bits by the vine snake, not to mention the essences extinction of the human race. Or suck it up, climb back onto the podium, hold off the vine snake *(only God knows how)*, and wait for Edison to rescue her. She chose to suck it up and remain in the fight. After all, Edison had probably already rescued the boat, and was on his way to help her.

Ellie pushed the crystals up onto the podium, and slowly pulled herself up. She never thought she'd be grateful for those gym class fitness tests, but today, it was the pull up portion that saved her life. She scrambled to her feet, and grabbed the crystals. She looked down the steps and screamed. The vine snake had slithered up and with its back arched like a cobra, was ready to strike. Riding on the back of the snake, like a rodeo cowboy, and grinning from ear to ear was Twig. The snake reared back in an effort to add more power to its strike. Ellie tried to scream, but the only sound that escaped her panicked body was a squeak. Her body went limp, and one of the crystals slipped out of her hands.

"Noooooooo!" Twig screamed in horror.

The crystal landed with a loud clank at Ellie's feet. A small chip, the size of a Hershey's kiss, broke off and rolled down the steps. Ellie followed it with her eyes as it bounced. Step after step, after step. Until it rolled to a halt against the thick woven body of the vine snake. The red crystal fragment flickered once as its glow faded and then turned black. The snake wasn't attacking; in fact, it looked to be backing up a bit. A small portion of vines on the snake's body withered, dried up, and fell away. Twig, on the back of the vine snake, had a hand clasped over his fanged mouth and seemed to be pleading with his eyes. It didn't take Ellie long to realize what had struck such terror in the Vines. The crystals were obviously much more than ballots for voting. Somehow, each of the essences were connected to their crystal. Which also explained why Lyvx was so scared when she had the Plants' crystal. *I wonder if it's a life-force thing? Oh, well . . . mental note to ask Lyvx if I don't get crushed to a pulp by the vine snake.* Ellie pushed the thought out of her head, too much was already going on.

She picked up the crystal that had fallen, and held it out over the edge of the podium. The vine snake backed up several feet. Ellie couldn't help but smile. She had found the vicious creature's weakness. Perhaps she WOULD make it out of this alive. She shook her outstretched hand, and the vine snake backed down, and off the podium. *Yes.* The gears, sprockets and springs of her mind spun like a cyclone. *Back the snake up. Get off the podium. Tell the Council about Twig's deception, and how he had them scare off the Ice Giants. Edison shows up, corroborates the story. Hopefully, Lyvx and the trees speak up, put in a few nice words about the human race. They vote again, everyone's crystal turns blue. Twig is smiling. Edison whisks me off and we go . . . aw crap! Why is Twig smiling!*

Indeed Twig, the nasty, little root man, was smiling. His eyes, once filled with horror, were now filled with delight and focused on something far behind her. Ellie slowly turned to look. "Aw crud!"

A dozen soil beasts stood on the edge of the lava pit with the fishing boat raised high above their heads. With little or no effort, they leaned forward and flung the boat into the pit. *NO!* A few long and agonizing seconds passed as disbelief and reason fought with each other in Ellie's mind. *This couldn't be happening*, she thought. After losing her grandmother and sister, now this. A large smoke cloud billowed out of the pit and filled the sky. Ellie screamed, or at least she thought she had. All she could hear was Twig's cackling laughter.

ROOT MAN

20.   A FAMILIAR VOICE

Ellie dropped to her knees. The never-ending stream of smoke billowing from the pit was accompanied by a thunderous symphony of hisses. Ellie figured it must be the sound of the vine snake's laughter, which would be attacking any second now. She made no attempt to fight. She had reached her physical and mental limit. It was over. She was drained.

The hissing was deafening, but it was not coming from the vine snake, which was behind her. *Where was it coming from*? She thought, *the forest, the council, the trees, Lyvx, the water falls . . . the pit?* Three different things came together in Ellie's mind at once. The first; the hissing noise was coming from the pit, deep down in its bowels to be exact. The second; the billowing smoke coming from the pit wasn't charred black, it was white. White and clear, like steam. *Steam?* And finally, her third and final realization; rising slowly in the center of the pit was the top of a young, brown haired boy's head. It was Edison, and he was standing on top of his stepfather's fishing boat, which was rising up out of the pit. Ellie sprang to her feet.

Edison gave Ellie a sheepish wave, and mouthed the words "Sorry." Ellie was too shocked to mouth anything back. She stood there silently, with her mouth hung open, as the fishing boat rose up out of the pit. Underneath the boat was a large bubbling wave of water. Edison had pulled a stream of water out from the waterfall ring, and used it to flood the pit and lift the boat. Ellie's dumbstruck look gave way to a faint smile, which made Edison blush ever so slightly. He hoped she didn't notice. And he was also hoping for another kiss on the check. The boat teetered slightly to the left, and Edison had to squint and gesture with his hands to regain control. Once the boat steadied, he gave Ellie a small "thumbs up" sign. He then pulled more water out from the falls, and using it like an arm, he lifted the boat up and over toward the waterfall ring surrounding the island. The soil beasts were beside themselves with anger as they watched Edison carry the boat away from the island toward the lake's surface. They clawed at the ground, reared back on their hind legs, and looked back toward the vine snake for guidance.

Ellie turned toward the vine snake as well. The crystals were once again outstretched in her hands, and this time she held them both out. Twig scowled, as she jiggled the crystals over the edge of the tall podium, high above the hard stone surface of the council circle. She couldn't help but smile. The vine snake slowly backed up from the stone podium, and far behind Ellie, the soil beasts withdrew from the pit. Higher and higher, Edison lifted the boat, as it slowly rose to the safety of the surface of the great lake. After so many trials and misfortunes, Edison and Ellie were finally able to breathe a hard earned sigh of relief. But as life goes, when so many things go right, something is bound to go wrong.

Ellie watched with beaming eyes, as the boy she helped encourage and inspire, lifted the fishing boat up and away from the submerged island. She smiled as she pictured Edison taking her in his arms and whisking her away from this dreadful place. And that's when it happened. While she was imaging the heart-warming look of defeat on Twig's face, she heard it. A low voice was calling out to her. A familiar voice.

"Ellie!"

21. CRACKLING

The boat stopped rising, and Ellie slowly pulled her arms, and the delicate crystals, back in and away from the podium's edge.

"Ellie."

Edison and Ellie answered in unison, "Viv!"

She stood at the foot of the podium, her golden blonde hair beaming like rays of sunshine, freshly plucked from the spinning orb of fire, so many millions of miles away. The brief moment of disbelief that Ellie felt, immediately gave way to joy in her heart. She ran down the tall stone steps to greet her sister. Edison stopped lifting the fishing boat, and slowly placed it down on the shore of the island. Neither Ellie nor Edison noticed that the nasty, little root man was smiling.

"Viv, oh my . . . how . . . where . . . you're alive!" Ellie threw her arms around her big sister and squeezed her tight.

"I . . . I don't know," answered Viv, apparently still shaking off the cobwebs of being dead. She looked around at the essences of the Council. Her eyes lingered on the soil beasts making their way back toward their platform, and then moved on to the fishing boat which rested safely on the island's sandy shore. Edison stepped down from the upper deck and gave Viv a wave. He was as happy to see Viv as Ellie was. And quite possibly for his own selfish reasons, he was a little bit more so. He'd been tortured by his failure to save her. Every time he shut his eyes, haunting images of the quicksand walls crashing down onto her filled the dark void. Edison's smile stretched ear to ear at the sight of Viv, and she smiled back. But it wasn't the type of smile Edison expected, it was something wicked.

Edison wanted to call out and warn Ellie, but he found himself frozen like a deer in the headlights of a speeding locomotive. What happened next, Edison watched helplessly and in slow motion. Viv pulled back from Ellie's hug, smiled, and then gently reached out and grasped both of her little sister's hands and the crystals held within them. Ellie tried to pull back, but her sister's grasp was too strong. Viv's nails transformed and turned into railroad spikes, which she plunged into the back of Ellie's hands. Ellie whimpered at hearing the cracking of the twenty-seven bones in each hand. Then, with almost no effort at all, Vivian took the two crystals away from her sister. Ellie lifted her fractured hands, now crumpled like the discarded wrappers of fast food hamburgers, and looked at her older sister's face. It was hard to tell which shone brighter, Viv's golden hair, or the twisted and wicked crescent of her menacing grin. Vivian lifted the crystals in a taunting gesture in front of Ellie's face and then, with the force of a Mac truck, leaned back and gave her little sister a kick. Edison watched as Viv's foot changed form and sprang out like a boxer's jab. The transformation gave her kick, and its impact, an excessive amount of force. Ellie flew through the air like a rag doll. Edison traced the path of her flight to a giant stone outcropping, which rose up from the island like a pylon. He reached out to her, willing a wall of water to cushion her impact. As the water raced up from the shallow depths of the surrounding shore, it sputtered and splashed to a halt well short of the stone pylon patiently waiting to flatten Ellie. Several clay soldiers rose up from the ground and blocked Edison's stream of water. WHAM! Ellie slammed into the stone pylon like a bug on the windshield of a Greyhound bus. The bones in her body cracked like brand flakes in a cereal box that had been stepped on by an elephant. Ellie fell to the ground.

"Ellie!" As Edison screamed, something deep within him urged much more than his voice forward. With the power and force of a fireman's hose, a large stream of water shot out from the waterfall ring surrounding the island, flew past Edison, and slammed right into the pearly grin of evil Viv. She quit smiling, dropped both crystals, and ever so slowly, the water washed away her body. The beautiful young girl, who once so proudly touted that she was made of sugar, spice and everything nice, was no longer flesh and bone. She was a soil creature, and as Edison's jets of water pummeled her, it was like watching the waves on a beach erode a sand castle. She tried to fight it, but as she raised her arms they were crumbled by the weight of her water soaked form.

Edison continued to scream as the jets of water shot past him. He lost himself in his anger, and wasn't sure if he had been screaming for seconds or hours. Slowly he became aware of the wet spray splashing his face, the violent sound of his own voice, the raw power of the water, and the gentle hand resting on his shoulder. He looked up and found the solemn face of Lyvx. Edison stopped screaming and hung his head. His heart was still racing and his lungs heaved as he tried to catch his breath. The jet spray of water slowly sputtered out.

Lyvx walked Edison over to Ellie's body. There were several small bushes scampering around her, examining her wounds, and gently brushing her with their leafy foliage. The small dandelion-man from the hilltop, held her hand. Ellie's chest convulsed as she fought for each gurgled breath. Edison knelt down beside her and delicately wiped the blood from her face.

"Is she . . . ?" Edison's words trailed off.

"No, but within minutes she will be," answered Lyvx.

"Is there anything we can do?" Edison turned and looked up at the talking tree. Lyvx, who in his young age had spawned close to a thousand saplings, looked down at Edison with all the warmth, compassion, and sadness of a father. Lyvx didn't make a sound, yet his eyes spoke of the deep sadness he felt in his core.

The sound of Ellie's breathing slowed with each weakened beat of her heart. The shrubs stopped their examination and stood still. The dandelion-man let out a small cry, as it buried its small head into the folds of Ellie's clothes, sniffling with each woeful sob. A dark shadow crept over Ellie's body. Edison looked up into the empty blackness of the mediator's dark hooded face. She bent down over Ellie and leaned in close to her. A thin, old hand reached out from the sleeve of the dark red robe, and brushed the stray hairs from Ellie's forehead. From high on the hill, the mediator seemed as stoic and cold as the stone podium on which she stood, but standing before Edison, she radiated warmth.

"Heh, heh," far off in the distance, but loud enough to be heard, was the sound of laughter. Edison whipped his head around. It didn't take him long to find the source of the heckling. Seated atop the podium was Twig. Kicking his feet like a kid seated on the edge of a swimming pool, and waving his hand like a beauty queen. The root man lifted up his crystal and smiled. Lyvx tightened his hold on Edison, sensing that the boy was going to run, but Edison quite literally slipped through Lyvx's fingers. His shoulder took a blue-ish liquid form, allowing him to slip through Lyvx's hold. The tree took curious note of the water dripping from his branches as Edison ran off.

"There must always be three . . . never two," said the mediator, as the shrubs crowded around Ellie. They fanned out, and then spread themselves over the young girl's body.

As Edison charged toward Twig, several water funnels rose up along the shore. The dark torrent of water twisted and churned as the anger and hatred boiled inside him. Impressed by the boy's talents, Twig gave a nod but made no attempt to run. Instead, the nasty, little root man calmly reached out his hand in a taunting "come-and-get-it" gesture. Edison screamed like a banshee, clenched his fists, and dove. The water funnels bent sharply at their bases and shot out like battering rams. The collision was sure to smash Twig to bits, and send root fragments all over the island. Spit flew from Edison's mouth, and tears ran from his eyes as the rushing water of the funnels joined up with him. SPLAT.

"Heh, heh," Twig couldn't help but giggle. SPLAT. SPLAT. A giant fist of tightly packed and condensed soil rose up and hammered down onto Edison's limp body. His charge had been stopped while in mid-air. The giant hammer-hand had struck out of nowhere. And with every blow, water spurted from every pore in Edison's body. SPLAT. SPLAT. The power of each blow struck with enough force to shatter every bone in his body. But instead of hearing the sharp crackling sound of splintered bones, there was only SPLAT. This was another curious side effect of Edison's aquatic condition. The solid state of his body's form gave way to liquid, and splattered with every blow. Not only did Edison have control over water, he was turning into it. SPLAT. SPLAT. In between blows, he was able to look up and trace the arm of the hammer-hand back to its owner. The giant, hammer-hand made out of tightly packed soil belonged to a very angry and wet blonde girl. Evil Viv lifted her giant hammer-hand up and smiled at the water dripping from it. SPLAT. For a moment Edison stuck to the under side of her fist before dripping off helplessly into a puddle. "Oh no, don't stop yet. Please . . . keep going," giggled Twig, "keep going!"

SPLAT. SPLAT. Evil Viv smiled, as her oddly shaped and enormously giant fist drove down and splattered what was left of Edison into scattered water droplets. The small army of soil beasts and clay soldiers standing behind the blonde soil-girl roared their approval. She lifted her giant fist for all to see. Water dripped down like rain. And then for show, Evil Viv gave the ground where Edison once laid, a final triumphant pound. There was no longer enough water to create a splat, only one last THUD. Edison was gone. All that remained was a pile of wet clothes and a small puddle of water. CLAP. CLAP. CLAP.

"Now that's what I call a show!" Twig stood up, clapped, and wiped the tears from his eyes. He had been laughing so hard during Edison's beating that his eyes started to swell. "Oh, the human race . . . how I will miss thee," he chucked as he and Evil Viv turned back toward the council circle, "NOT!"

23. LOOK UP

Twig hummed a delightfully awful, little tune as he went about his work. With great care, and much satisfaction, he placed each of the seven crystals back into their slots on the floor of the Great Council. He gently lowered the crystal of the Clays into its slot, looked up, and gave a friendly wave to the crowd of clay soldiers gathered on their platform. He carefully lifted the Vine's crystal, wiped off a piece of dirt, and ever so gently lowered it into its slot. The vine snake coiled on its platform. It hissed its approval, to which Twig politely bowed in response. The next two crystals, Fresh Water and Salt Water, were dropped into their slots without care. Both pools of water were as placid as ever; neither the rescue of the fishing boat or the demise of Edison caused the slightest ripple. Twig paused a moment with the crystal of the Plants. He looked up and saw Lyvx glaring at him with his branches crossed. Seated on the edge of the platform, and quite angry, was the dandelion-man, who shook a pedal fist at Twig. The nasty, little root man smiled and dropped the plant crystal. CLANK. It fell on the ground and bounced just to the right of its slot. "Oops!" He then turned and kicked the crystal into its slot. Lyvx gave a disapproving grunt, as the trees behind him stirred.

Next was the Soils' crystal, which Twig presented to Vivian like a royal messenger would hand a rolled parchment to a queen. Vivian graciously took the crystal, making a show of the process, bent down and gently placed it into its slot. She proudly stood up, chin held high, and strode like a fashion model on the runway back to the platform of the Soils. The soil beasts reared back and applauded their newest recruit, Evil Viv. They welcomed her with open arms. Twig did a little shimmy and shake, something resembling that of a end-zone-dance, as he scooted his way over to the slot of the final crystal. He shot a smile back over his shoulder toward Lyvx, and nonchalantly let the Ice Giants' crystal roll off his fingertips and fall into its slot. He positioned and readied himself to give the plants a tauntingly evil wink as he waited for the final crystal to clank into its hole. He waited. And waited. And waited. There was no clank. Lyvx was no longer glaring, and the dandelion-man was no longer shaking an angry pedal. In fact, Twig thought that it almost looked like the Plants were smiling.

As his concern grew, he looked down at the slot by his feet. The slot was empty, and hovering just a few inches above the slot was the final crystal, wrapped tightly in a bouquet of red roses. "Huh?" Twig watched, as his jaw hung open. The bouquet of red roses lifted the crystal up to his face. The roses and crystal moved right under his crooked little nose. The sweet scent of the roses made him recoil and gag in disgust. And as the bouquet began to pull back from Twig, the rose pedals turned into fingers. The fingers then joined a small palm to form a young girl's hand with ruby red nail polish. As his eyes moved up from the crystal, Twig noticed that there was a young girl holding it. "No way!"

"Yes way!" Ellie gave the nasty, little root man the sweetest little southern-belle-smile she could muster. With her right hand firmly grasped around the Ice Giants' crystal, she slowly twirled her left hand, as her fingertips sprouted rose pedals. The sight captivated Twig. "Pretty, huh?" ask Ellie.

"How did – uh oh," Twig gulped. Ellie's smile turned from sweet to salty. Her dainty, little pink and rose tipped hand turned the dark, green shade of rose stems, and a dozen very large, sharp thorns appeared. Ellie's entire body then turned dark green as she moved her thorn-covered hand across and through Twig, slashing his twisted root body to shreds. A collective gasp echoed across the circle of the Great Council. Never before had they witnessed the fusion of their essence and humans. And now, within the span of minutes, they were bearing witness to three such beings.

Evil Viv: part human and part soil
Edison: part human and part fresh water
Ellie: part human and part plant.

The vine snake coiled back and rose with a menacing HISS. Unsure of this new adversary, it didn't know if it should attack or turn tail and run. "Mary, Mary quite contrary. How does your garden grow?" Vivian calmly stepped down from the Soils' platform, and onto the floor of the Great Council. "I like

90

what you've done with yourself El. It's about time you added some color to that dank wardrobe of yours." While her words smacked of sarcasm, Ellie immediately identified the challenge in her sister's tone and stance. The army of clay soldiers marched down from their platform, and gathered rank behind Vivian. A small, heckling hint of laughter could be heard in the great vine snake's hiss. "Oh, you just missed the little bait boy . . . I think he wet himself." Vivian's smile curled up like a viper's snarl. Ellie's brow wrinkled as she suppressed a small internal growl. Rival siblings, especially sisters, have the ability to push each other's buttons in nano-seconds. Clearly, Vivian was a master of this art. "Round two, lil' sis?"

The vine snake slide down from its platform, and rose up behind Evil Viv and the clay soldiers. The numbers were in her favor. She struck a particularly sassy pose, crossed her arms, and flashed Ellie the type of grin you'd like to knock off her face with a baseball bat. Ellie simmered like a boiling teakettle. She clenched her slightly sweaty fists, and prepared to blow her top. It would be hopeless for her to challenge the combined forces of Evil Viv, the vine snake, the clay soldiers, and the soil beasts. But she was determined to slap that tauntingly fake grin from her sister's perfect, dimpled face. It probably wouldn't even be much of a fight. Evil Viv would get the final crystal, and the human race would be sentenced to extinction. But if she could just get her hands around her sister's throat for a few seconds . . . it would be worth it. With the flair and panache that only a beautiful, big sister could have, Evil Viv blew her awkward, little sister a kiss. Ellie blew her top.

"Oh, that's i—," Ellie took the first step of her charge, and then froze in her tracks.

"Er, er, errrrr!" Ellie looked down and watched as all 14 inches of the little dandelion-man stomped toward her, his pedals clenched like fists, to stand by her side. The sudden show of support was enough to cool Ellie's temper. Help, no matter how big or how small, was still help, and it was greatly appreciated.

"Uh–hem!" The rough bark of a large branch-hand lowered, and gave Ellie's shoulder a pat. Lyvx, several large oak trees, and shrubs stepped down from their platform to stand behind Ellie. As she looked up at the tall oaks, Lyvx greeted her with a comforting nod. While it was quite difficult to make out any of the expressions on the Lyvx's face, the look she now saw reminded her of her father. It was the look that her father gave her when she won the school spelling bee in second grade, the blue ribbon at the district science fair, and the same look he gave Vivian when she was voted prettiest hair on the junior cheerleading squad. It was a look she missed, and might never see again. While both parents were only 50 yards away, they lay unconscious on the fishing boat with the rest of their condemned shipmates. So much had happened in the last twenty-four hours. The giant wave, her grandmother's death, the submerged island, the bait boy with super-water-powers, the nasty, little root man, the vine snake, talking trees, Vivan's supposed death, her own near-death, the vote that condemned mankind, some kind of fusion with the plant essence, and now this stand off.

Lyvx's large, brown, wooden eyes blinked and returned Ellie's thoughts to her current predicament. She was happy to see that Lyvx's comforting look was still there. It gave her the little bit of extra confidence she needed to calm her heels, and muster a small smile, even though the odds were clearly against them. If this were a college football game, Evil Viv's team would have been favored over Ellie's team by at least 46 points.

"Ok sis, here's the deal . . . march your little butt over here, hand me the crystal, and we'll only smack you and your plant buddies around a little bit." Vivian smiled and crossed her arms, like a prosecuting attorney. "Final offer."

"Hmmm, I don't know . . . what do you think Edison?"

Edison? A few brief moments passed while everyone at the Great Council exchanged confused looks. Even Lyvx nervously looked at Ellie, perhaps the stress of the day had gotten to her. Everyone saw Vivian pound Edison into a puddle of water, so what could she be up to?

"Edison?" repeated Ellie, this time a little bit louder.

"Oh uh, hey . . . Ellie . . . you're OK, that's . . . uh . . . that's great." Ellie looked over and saw Edison's head sticking up out of a puddle of water. His head was blue and semi-transparent. Edison's body was no longer flesh and bone. It was made out of glowing blue water. Ellie thought he looked like he

92

was made out of Berry Blue Jell-O. Edison lifted a blue hand up out of the puddle and reached for his shirt and shorts. "Ah hem!"

"Oh, sorry," Ellie turned away as a naked blue Edison climbed up out of the puddle and pulled on his clothes. The crowd was silent and they watched in wonder as the water from the puddle was soaked up to form Edison. After buttoning his shorts, he walked over and stood next to Ellie. A small step behind her actually.

"I ah . . . I wasn't hiding," whispered Edison. Ellie gave him a smile, knowing full well that he was hiding. The little dandelion-man looked up at Edison and gave him a spiteful grunt. "I wasn't!"

"What's it gonna be Ellie?" Vivan spat out from across the circle.

"We're not really going to fight them are w-" before Edison was able to finish his sentence Ellie answered back.

"I'm sorry Vivian, I must not have been listening . . . what was your offer again?" Ellie asked.

"Oh, that's great. Piss off the dirt girl with the big, hammer fists. Did you see what she -ow!" Ellie jabbed her elbow into Edison's ribs. It did the job, and shut him up. Apparently, even in his new blue form, he was still firm enough to feel the pain of a jab.

Sigh! Vivian's sigh was purposely loud and dramatic. "OK, how about this . . . give me the crystal, or I'll squash you like a bug!"

Ellie answered right away this time. "Oh yeah, that's right . . . now I remember. Sorry, must be that whole smashing me into a rock thing you did." Ellie smiled and shrugged her shoulders. "Do you mind if I take a second and discuss it with my friends."

"What?!?!"

"Well . . . YOU ARE condemning the entire human race here," Ellie motioned to the Great Council around her, "I figure it's worth at least a minute or two?" Edison lowered his head and slapped his blue forehead in disbelief. Ellie smiled as pleasantly as she could, and prayed that she was able to hide the sarcasm in her body language. "Pretty please, Viv!"

93

Vivian huffed loudly. Clearly her little sister's request had taken her by surprise. Her face wrinkled, visibly under the duress of trying to think hard and quickly. Which was something new for the prettiest little girl in Abraham Lincoln Junior High. "One minute! And not a second more!" *What is that stupid little brat up to?!?!*

"Thanks big sis! You're the best!" Ellie turned back toward her team, and huddled them up. Edison, Lyvx, the dandelion-man, and the rest of the plants gathered around her.

"I wasn't hiding."

"Yeah, we know," Ellie brushed off Edison's words, while the dandelion-man folded his pedals and grunted his disapproval.

"I wasn't." While no one was looking, Lyvx reached out a branch and gently poked at Edison's glowing blue body. "Hey, quit it!"

Lyvx was surprised to see that Edison's body was indeed solid, "hmmmm." A small drop of water fell from his branch.

"OK, here's the plan." Ellie waved everyone in the huddle closer together. "I think the best thing for us to do is get THIS crystal," Ellie held up the crystal in her hand, "as far away from HERE as possible."

"Perhaps we could then hide it, until we are able to present a better case before the Council," said Lyvx. The plants and trees around him nodded their approval.

"Yeah, cause you guys did such a good- OW!" Ellie once again jammed an elbow into Edison's rib cage.

"Good thinking, Lyvx!" the young girl answered quickly in an effort to cut Edison off.

While Ellie huddled her team, Evil Viv's group grew anxious. A small rumbling started to build amongst the clay soldiers. Vivian cocked an eyebrow, turned and then beckoned the vine snake to her side. She whispered a few quick words to the snake, smiled a sweetly, vicious smile, and pointed up toward the waterfalls that circled the island. The vine snake gave a little chuckle of a hiss, as it slithered off into the jungle.

Edison was the only one on his team to notice the vine snake sneak off. And the only reason he noticed it was because he was staring at Vivian instead of listening to Ellie's plan. "Uh

94

oh . . . ah Ellie," Edison tapped Ellie on the shoulder. "The ah . .
. vine sna- . ."

"Shush. Edison, you better be paying attention."

"But the vine-"

"EDISON, we're trying to save the human race, OK. If
you could focus for one minute, 8 billion people would REALLY
appreciate it." Edison opened his mouth once more, but quickly
shut it after he saw the look on Ellie's face. The dandelion-man
huffed loudly and rolled his eyes.

"Alright, to get the crystal away from the island, we need
to distract Vivian and the vine snake. I don't think the clay
soldiers have the ability to pursue anyone, and I have no idea
where those soil beasts went."

Edison was the first one to volunteer for duty. "I'll
distract the vine snake." And the only reason he did so was
because he knew something the others did not.

"Really?"

"Really?" added Lyvx. The other trees added something
that must have also meant *"really,"* in their own language.

"Well . . . thank you," Ellie had to pause a moment to
process Edison's request. "But . . . with my new abilities, I think
I might be a little more adapt to handle the vine snake." Ellie
raised her hand. It quickly turned green and sprouted long, sharp
spikes.

"Bummer." *So much for getting the easy part of this
group project,* thought Edison. "How about Vivian, can I take
her?"

"Yeah, cause that worked out really well for you last
time," said Lyvx, without missing a beat. Edison shot the tree a
look.

"She did kind of smash you into a puddle," said Ellie.

"Yeah, well," Edison's eyes bounced from Ellie to Lyvx
and back again, "she's cute."

*That's it . . . she's toast. Like twenty minutes ago, I gave
him a kiss, which, by the way, made him speechless. And SHE
calls him names, SHE smashes him into the ground, SHE tries to
kill him, wants to wipe out the entire human race, AND HE'S
STILL head over heels in love with her! What the heck, man?!?!*

95

What do I have to do to get out of the shadow of her enormously huge, blonde head? "She calls you bait boy!"

Ellie's sudden outburst caused Edison to lean back out of the huddle. "Huh?"

"Nothing, look . . . the trees can handle Vivian-"

"But I really think I-" Edison's protest was cut short.

"NO. The trees will handle my sister. You're the fastest. You need to take the crystal and . . ." Ellie's words trailed off when she looked down at her feet.

"And what?" asked Edison. Ellie ignored his question. The group was soon covered in darkness as a huge shadow slowly crept over top of them and blocked out the sun. Ellie watched as the shadow moved across the floor of the council, and then finally stopped three inches from Vivian's bubblegum pink, painted toenails. Vivian stood as sassy as ever, with her hands firmly planted on her hips. She then gave Ellie, the most sarcastic what-ever-could-that-be look she could muster. And then Evil Viv pointed up.

As Ellie looked up, her jaw dropped. The rest of her group had the same reaction.

"I think we need a new plan," said Edison.

24. THUD SMASH THUD

THUD. Edison, Ellie, and Lyvx were frozen as the first one fell. THUD. THUD. By the time the third one fell, Edison found his scream. "Ahhhhhhhhhhhh!" THUD. When the fourth one fell, Edison turned and ran. THUD. THUD. Before the seventh one fell, Ellie had grabbed Edison's ankle with her transformed-stretched-out-ivy-arm, and had dragged him back to her side. THUD.

"Ahhhhhhh!" Lyvx picked Edison and Ellie up in his branches, and dove to the right. THUD. Edison looked back to where they had been standing, and saw a very large, and very heavy, steel-shipping container. *Gulp.* Had Lyvx not scooped them up, Edison and Ellie would have been squashed like grapes. THUD. THUD. Large steel shipping containers (yellow, black, and blue) were now falling from the sky like raindrops. THUD. THUD. Hanging high above the council circle was the bow end of a large industrial Great Lakes shipping freighter. The boat was teetering on the edge of the waterfall ring that surrounded the submerged island. As the freighter tipped, shipping containers broke loose, slid across the deck, and then out over the ship's side. THUD. THUD. The current from the falls pushed the front of the ship further and further out into the air above the submerged island.

As far as Edison was concerned, two-ton steel boxes falling from the sky qualified for an "every-man-for-himself" approach. He twisted out of Lyvx's branches and ran for the jungle.

"Edison! Wait!" Ellie called out.

"No! You run too!"

"The boat! They'll crush the boat!"

"Who cares, I hate that boat!"

"But my parents are on it!" Edison reached the edge of the jungle and stopped running. "And we need your help!" He turned and looked back at Ellie. She was lying on the ground underneath Lyvx, who swatted away a falling shipping container that was about to hit them. Pushing away the container cracked and twisted several of the few remaining branches that Lyvx had left. Edison gulped as he watched tears form at the corners of

Ellie's eyes. It felt as if someone had punched him in the gut with a sledgehammer.

Don't do it. Don't do it. Don't do it. You've been a chicken all your life, and it's gotten you this far. Edison bit his lip and it dissolved into water. *Don't do it.* Edison looked up and watched as a shipping container slammed into the side of the freighter's railing directly above the small fishing boat. *Don't do it.* Steel bolts snapped and flew out of the railing as it gave way to the steel container's weight. *Don't do it. You HATE that stupid, smelly, rotten, dirty boat.* Ellie closed her eyes, and dropped her head. Edison turned back toward the jungle. *She did kiss me . . . and that was cool.* The freighter's railing broke and dropped the container like a bomb. *AND . . . her sister's smoking hot. What the heck!*

BOOM! The sound echoed across the island, and wiped the smile off of Evil Viv's pursed lips. Edison imagined himself as a jet of water, shooting across the council circle like water from a fire hose, and slamming into the falling container with the force of a cement truck going 150 mph. It happened exactly as he imagined. Edison smashed into the side of the container, folded it like a pop can, and used the momentum of the collision to push it off to the side and redirect himself up toward the drooping freighter. Water from the shallow pools around the island rose up under Edison like a pillar, and pushed him toward the ship's hull. He hit the bottom of the boat at full speed and it stopped him dead in his tracks. It turns out that a 1,000-foot Great Lakes freighter, filled with roughly 300 steel shipping containers, weighed about as much as you'd think it would. Edison groaned as the water pillar rising below him pancaked him up against the bottom of the boat.

"Go Edison, go! You can do it!" Ellie called out from the island below. *Is she cheering for me? No one EVER cheers for me. They yell at me a lot. Edison clean up this! Edison wipe up that! Edison why did you do that? Edison shut up and cut more bait! Edison why are you so stupid? No wonder no one ever adopted you.* Ellie's voice called out again, and separated him from his current line of thought. "We believe in you!" *Yep, she is cheering for me. Heck even that little, yellow, flower-looking-weed-dude is cheering for me. This is so cool!*

Edison pushed himself back from the ship's hull, repositioned his grip, and gritted his teeth. Water sprang from the falls and added to the pillar rising up under him. It took a few moments, and several thousand gallons of lake water, but he was able to stop the descent of the boat. And ever so slowly, like a jack underneath the left rear tire of a car, Edison lifted the freighter. Ellie thought he looked like the mythical Greek hero Atlas, rising with the world upon his shoulders. *Well, a glowing blue, much younger, and less muscular version of the Greek Hero.* Vivian folded her arms, and huffed with a pout similar to the time she was runner-up in the Little Miss Harvest pageant.

At the pageant, when the newly christened "Little Miss Harvest" stepped forward to accept her crown, Vivian stuck out a foot and "accidentally" tripped her. And now it was time Edison, "Little Miss Bait Boy," was tripped too.

As Vivian pulled back her hand, it turned from fleshy pink to dark, gritty dirt, and then took the shape of a large scythe blade. With her new weapon slung back like a bat, Vivian ran off to swat Edison. She only got two steps before . . . SMACK! A large tangle of branches struck Vivian right across the bridge of her nose, and she flew back like a rag doll. She rolled and bounced a few times before coming to a stop forty yards away, face down in the dirt. Scowling, she lifted her head, tossed her disheveled hair to the side, and looked up. The first thing she saw was her little sister, grinning from ear-to-ear. Ellie gave her big sis a taunting, pinky wave. Vivian growled. Ellie stopped waving with her pinky finger and pointed it straight up in the air, paused a moment, and then bent it down sharply. The tall tree behind Vivian bent the same way that Ellie's pinky finger did, and smashed down on top of Vivian. WHAM! "Look, sis, I've got powers too!" said Ellie with a smile. "Tee-hee!" Apparently Ellie's new powers also included controlling plants, and the large club-like-trees, around her.

Vivian reached her hands out, and dug her fingernails deep into the dirt in front of her. A wall of earth rose up behind Ellie like a giant wave. By the time Ellie figured out why her sister was smiling it was too late. The wall of dirt behind Ellie rose up, spread out, and covered her like a 643-pound dirt blanket. Now it was Vivian's turn to give Ellie a pinky wave. "Tee hee, grrrrr!"

Lyvx immediately rushed over to rescue Ellie. But just as the tall tree dug his branches into the dirt, three clay soldiers jumped onto his back. The battle royal was underway. The trees and the plants wrestled with the clay soldiers and soil beasts as various mounds of dirt rose up and dumped down on just about anything that moved. Vivian hit Ellie with wave after wave of dirt, and Ellie in return kept hammering Vivian with the club-like-trees behind her. All the while, the pools of fresh water and salt water sat motionless. The raging battle before the others caused not the slightest ripple in their placid pools. Equally neutral was the mediator, who stood and watched silently from her podium. She was forbidden to interfere with conflicts between the Earth's Essences.

Ellie was still holding the last crystal clutched tightly to her chest. She twisted and slashed at the battery of dirt and mud hands seeking to pluck the prize from her. The arrangement of the battle wasn't quite what Ellie had hoped for, but it was providing a very nice distraction. She wasn't sure how long it would go unnoticed, but Edison was still raising the ship. Not only was it no longer raining shipping containers, but the freighter had leveled off, and Edison was pushing it back from the falls. The small fishing charter of Edison's foster dad was no longer in danger. All the people sleeping aboard, including Ellie and Vivian's parents, were out of harm's way . . . at least for the moment.

25.　THE BLIND SQUIRREL

Holy crap! I'm doing it! I'm actually doing it! As
Edison lifted the freighter, brilliant moments of what were sure to
be his glory days flashed through his head. It was like he was
running down the field, ready to score the winning touchdown
and bring home the State Championship for his school. Or at
least this was how he imagined it felt. He really wasn't the most
coordinated boy on the block. He was nine before he learned
how to hit a baseball, and was almost eleven before he took the
training wheels off of his bike, which didn't do much for his
street cred. Sports weren't really his thing. And up until this
very moment, he didn't think he even had a "thing." But now he
was contemplating joining his school's swim team.

Occasionally, the boat would slide back a bit as Edison
snuck quick peeks at the battle below. It was pretty much a
stalemate. The sisters, Ellie and Evil Viv, were taking turns
smacking each other, neither gaining more then a brief advantage
over the other. Lyvx and the trees kept the clay soldiers at bay,
despite their increasing numbers. Every time one of the trees
smashed a clay soldier, it would split into two new soldiers. The
little green shrubs did their best to herd most of the soil beasts off
toward the beach or back into the jungle. Eventually, the tide of
the battle might favor Vivian and her nasty, little team. But by
that time Edison would have the boat safely away from the falls,
and be entering the fray himself. With his help, Ellie and the
plants would easily win. Of course, there still was that tiny little
matter of the council's vote, but he didn't worry much about it.
He was sure Ellie would have a plan for that. *Note to self, be
sure to rescue her first, might get another kiss!* A few more
minutes and the freighter would be a safe distance back from the
falls, and then it would be bad guy (and bad girl) butt whooping
time! *Hmm, this isn't that tough. I wonder why I didn't do this
earlier?*

The answer to Edison's question came in the form of a
very large object slamming into his ribs. His stomach collapsed,
as everything went black. He could feel himself flying back
through the air, and then free falling. He fought to open his eyes,
and just as he did . . . he wished he hadn't. The first thing he saw

was the gigantic open jaw of the vine snake. It pounced down on him like a venomous, emerald green adder. And just behind the great snake, was a large, black, rectangular shape. The freighter was creeping out over the falls once more. Edison felt worse than ever. Like every other "almost-moment-of-glory" in his life, he had fumbled the ball inches from the goal line. But this time, something was different. It wasn't much but it was something. Instead of feeling the weight of his 99.7% failure rate, he saw the light of his .3% success rate. And he felt it, in the memory of Ellie's warm kiss on his cheek. *By golly if I can't be the receiver who scores the winning touchdown, than I'll be the blind squirrel who finds the nut!*

The jaws of the vine snake must have been moving at 300 miles per hour when they snapped shut. At the last second, Edison twisted out of the way. He grabbed onto the back of the snake's head, riding it downward like a missile, and summoned a plume of water from the falls. There was an explosion of water and sand when he and the vine snake crashed onto the shore of the submerged island. The speed and added weight of the water drove the vine snake's head deep into the muddy earth. Like a rubber ball falling from the sky, Edison rebounded and flew back up toward the freighter. *Go blind squirrel, go!* He hit the boat with so much force and confidence that it not only leveled the ship off, it raised the bow several feet into the air. He didn't have long to push though. Before he was even able to steady his grip, the vine snake was on him. While the great green Adler's head was still stuck in the dirt, what was once the tail morphed into another set of venomous jaws. *Oh great, a giant TWO headed vine snake. This trip just keeps getting better and better*, thought Edison as he tried to wiggle his legs free of the vines. The vine snake stretched out and twisted itself around him like a python. It quickly wrapped itself around his legs, waist, up over his back, and around his neck. The vine snake ripped him away from the hull of the freighter and down toward the island. The freighter rocked back toward the falls as several shipping containers slid over its side. THUD. THUD. THUD. They landed dangerously close to the fishing boat. Several more steel containers slid toward the edge of the freighter.

Aw, man! These vines can't hold me, aren't I supposed to be made out of water or something, thought Edison. *What the heck! What did I do when Vivian was pounding me? She is so beautiful. Wait . . . focus . . . focus. She smashed me into a puddle of water. Her beautiful, long, blonde hair blowing in the . . . FOCUS! I turned into a puddle. Did I do that or did she?* Edison's teeth rattled as he and the vine snake slammed back down onto the shore. *Ok, she's like made out of dirt now, so it had to be me.* He looked up to see the shadow of a falling shipping container. *Ahhhhh!* THUD. The vine snake rolled them out of the way just in time. Ok, so that's at least something good. *The giant, evil vine snake doesn't want to be squashed either. No, wait . . . maybe I do want to be squashed?* Edison struggled with the vines, but couldn't loosen their grip as they lifted him up and whipped him spastically through the air. Each time he struggled, the vines tightened their grip. THUD. THUD. *So much for finding that nut,* the blind squirrel thought to himself.

Fortunately, for Edison, he wasn't the only one who remembered being smashed into a puddle. True to form, Evil Viv paused to allow for adequate gloating time over her opponent. She relaxed her guard, flipped her hair, smiled, and planted her hands on her hips. And just as she opened her mouth to speak, Ellie planted a tree trunk sized fist right into Vivian's face. *Boy, I really hope she's possessed by the soils. 'Cause if not, she's like totally gone evil . . . well, evil for Viv at least,* thought Ellie as she spun and ran across the council circle toward Edison, the vine snake, and the fishing boat. THUD. She jumped, tucked, and rolled. THUD. Dodging the containers wasn't the only challenge. Apparently, several of the clay soldiers had been keeping an eye on her, and half a dozen broke off their attack on Lyvx and the trees to attack her. She dove through the hands of the first clay soldier, and jumped onto the back of the second. That caused the third clay soldier to crash into the second clay soldier. She transformed her hands into two green stemmed, thorny fists, and sliced the fourth and fifth clay soldiers into six or seven pieces each. But in doing so, Ellie lost sight of the sixth clay soldier. He was now behind her, with his clay fists clenched together high above his head. He swung them down like a wrecking ball. By the time Ellie turned, it was too late. The shadow of the impending doom had eclipsed her. High above in the air, Edison struggled to free himself, but all he could do was watch helplessly. As the clay soldier narrowed its eyes on its target, Ellie winced and shut her eyes. She was done for. THUD.

The gust of wind from the impact pushed back her hair. Slowly she opened one eye. Resting two inches from the tip of her nose was a large, steel shipping container. She opened her other eye and looked down. Sticking out from under the container was a pair of clay arms. It reminded her of the Wicked Witch of the East's feet in the Wizard of Oz, after Dorothy's house had landed on her. *Darn straight, there's no place like home!* For the first time since this adventure began, she wondered if she would ever see home again. But it was only for a moment. *Yes, I definitely will see home again!* She was something of a glass-half-full girl. *And so will mom and dad!* So Ellie clicked her heels together once, and dug her hands deep down into the ground under the shipping container. *And so will Vivian!* She groaned as her body turned green, and her arms thickened and transformed into tree trunks. With the aid of her new powers, she did the impossible. She lifted the very large, and very heavy, steel shipping container high above her head and took aim. *And so will Edison!* She heaved back, and threw.
Oh hey, wow look at that, thought Edison as the vine snake slammed him down onto the ground. *Ellie's lifting that huge shipping container all by herself . . . cool. I wish I could do that. Hey where's she throwing that – AHHHHHHHHHH!* THUD. The vine snake never saw the shipping container coming. As it smashed down onto the vine snake, water squirted out from under the great steel box. A puddle formed next to the container, from which Edison stuck up his head. As he pulled himself up and out of the puddle, he realized he was once again naked. Panicking to cover himself, he reached for his shorts and shirt. Even in his blue watery form, Ellie could tell he was blushing. THUD. THUD. Containers were falling all around them. "Edison! This is no time to be bashful!"
"But my-"

THUD. Ellie jumped out of the way of a container and right into a giant pair of dirt claws. Vivian squeezed tightly, intent on crushing her dear little sister like a grape. "Edison!"

Before Ellie's eyes disappeared under the claws of dirt, Edison saw her look of panic. Edison whipped around and saw two shipping containers falling down toward the fishing boat. "Aw crap!" Edison dropped his shirt, tucked his shorts under his arm, and took off like a jet of water toward the falling steel boxes. He hit the first hard, dented the side in, and knocked it just to the side of the boat. There was barely enough time for him to twist and kick out at the second container. He was only able to put enough force behind his strike to push the container three feet to the left. *Was it enough to miss the boat?* The steel box fell hard, and buckled under its own weight as it landed. THUD. He winced as he looked down. To his delight and amazement, he saw that the shipping container had landed right next to the boat. So close, it had even scrapped some paint off of the boat's side. *Wow, that was too close.* He dropped down onto the deck of his foster father's fishing boat, quickly pulled his shorts on, and looked up. The freighter was once again tipping down toward the submerged island. Trying his hardest to think like Ellie, he calculated that it would be at least three minutes before the boat would fall, one hundred and eighty seconds. Surely with that many seconds he could help Ellie and keep the freighter from falling. *One hundred and seventy-six . . . now or never!*

Edison clenched his fists and then shot both of his hands out toward Vivian, and her giant mound of dirt. The geyser of water caught her off guard, flipped her head over heels, and blasted her back across the council circle. *One hundred and sixty-one.* He redirected the water from the falls, and aimed it at the giant mound of dirt that was covering Ellie. Like the tide tearing down the ramparts of a child's sandcastle, the dirt mound gave way to Edison's jet stream. *One hundred and fifty-five seconds, come on . . . she has to be here somewhere.* He strengthened his effort, and pulled even more water from the falls. He didn't need to look up to check on the boat. He could see the shadow of the freighter creeping further out over the submerged island. *Crap! I can't – oh, arm! That's an arm! Is*

106

that an arm? Yes, it's an arm. His excitement at finally unearthing one of Ellie's body parts gave his jet stream of water just enough of an extra boost to blow the dirt away from her face. *One hundred and thirty-three seconds.* Edison washed the dirt away from the top half of Ellie's body, and shut off the flow of his water streams. Ellie's body slumped, as she fell back in the mud. "Ellie, Ellie!" yelled Edison.

Ellie's stomach jerked as she coughed up a lung full of lake water. "Are you OK?" Ellie rolled her eyes at Edison's ridiculous question. She did her best to hide her pain, lifted her hand, gave him a thumbs-up sign, and then pointed up toward the shipping freighter. THUD. A steel container landed just to the right of Edison. *Ok, time to switch focus.* "Hey Ellie, I kind of have to go now." Ellie impatiently waved for him to take off. Edison sent one last little blast of water to clean off Ellie's legs, and then turned his attention back toward the freighter.

He planted his feet, squatted down, looked up, and thought of Superman. *Up, up, and away!* Edison pushed off from the fishing boat's deck and flew up toward the hull of the freighter with his fists extended. *One hundred and twenty-nine seconds, plenty of time.* Water from the falls flew out and joined up with him to double the speed of his charge. He braced for impact, and closed his eyes. With a rough jolt, he came to an abrupt stop . . . but there was no impact. He opened his eyes and saw that he had stopped three feet from the bottom of the boat. He looked down at his waist and saw a thick, twisted, coil of dark green vines. Before he had time to react, the vines yanked him back hard, like a fisherman seeking to dig his hook deep in the lip of a "big catch." WHAM! He slammed back down onto the island. *One hundred and ouch . . . fifteen seconds.*

Edison quickly sat up. And as he did, he felt the weight of two heavy hands on his shoulders. He bent his head back and looked up. "Hello Bait-boy." Standing over him with a wide venomous grin was Evil Viv. The vine snake coiled up behind her like a bodyguard. Edison couldn't help but notice how nice her hair looked, especially after being blasted by a water cannon. THUD. THUD. Steel shipping containers were raining down all around them. He winced at the pain he felt in his shoulders. Vivian's long, manicured, passion-pink fingernails grew out like long spikes, which she dug into Edison's shoulders. The pain was so intense he could barely muster a whimper, let alone scream. *Ninety-nine seconds. Crap again!*

Edison tried to slap at Evil Viv's hands, and for his effort, he received the second largest dose of pain he'd ever experienced in his life . . . or so he thought. *Seventy-three seconds. Double crap! Why can't I just change back into water agai- OW!* Edison's neck jerked back involuntarily, as his jaw thrust open. Spit flew from his mouth. While his head was back, he noticed a very large steel container falling right toward them. Vivian was too busy savoring her kill to notice. *This is going to hurt . . . real bad.* Just as he was about to shut his eyes, he could feel Vivian's nails rip out of his shoulders as he slid through the mud. THUD. He tucked his head down into his chest, and missed the falling container by half an inch. The speed and weight of the container sunk it deep in the mud. There was no sign of Evil Viv. Edison put his hands over his chest in an effort to keep his heart from beating out of it. It felt like it was going to explode.

"The freighter," a very tired and familiar voice spoke the words. Standing before him, on a pair of wobbly legs, was Ellie. She'd spent the last of her energy pulling him from harm's way. It looked as if the faintest breeze would blow her over. To say she was exhausted would be an understatement. She fell down to her knees, and lacking the energy to speak, she pointed up toward the tipping freighter. *Fifty seconds.*

It was a strange phenomenon, but the mere site of Ellie gave Edison strength. Perhaps it was the magic spell bestowed on those who have given us our first kiss. Or perhaps it was the mysterious healing power of seeing someone who was significantly sicker than oneself. Either way, Edison jumped to his feet. He smiled, gave Ellie a quick thumb's up, and then shot up toward the freighter. The exploding, afterburner spray of water knocked Ellie back on her butt. *Forty-six seconds.*

Out of the corner of his eye, Edison saw the vine snake matching the speed of his ascent, and nearing to strike. *Forty-one seconds.* He had to go faster, if the vine snake caught him, the freighter would surely move beyond the point of no return. *Faster!* He looked to his right, and as suddenly as it had appeared, the vine snake disappeared. Edison looked back over his shoulder and saw a very exhausted Ellie, with her hands once again transformed into dark, green, thorn-covered, rose stems. Even though she lacked the strength to stand, she had somehow mustered enough energy to slash out at the vine snake and cut it in half. The effort depleted the last reserves of her energy. Just as Edison went to smile, he noticed Evil Viv sneaking up behind Ellie. Now her hair was quite disheveled and she looked very pissed off. Evil Viv lifted her hands as her nails grew out like pink, razor sharp spikes. *Thirty-nine seconds.* There was no way for Edison to warn her, and no time. He was too far away, and the roar of the falls was too loud. All he could do was hope Lyvx and the trees could save her. If he was to stop the freighter from falling, he would be powerless to help Ellie.

BOOM! Edison's impact with the freighter rang out and reverberated off of the hull of the boat like thunder. The freighter was now tipping downward at a 45-degree angle. *Thirty-seven seconds.* This time Edison's collision with the bottom of the hull didn't raise the freighter up out of the water. In fact it didn't raise the boat at all. He pushed with all his might, and urged more and more water up from the falls and shore around the submerged island. THUD. THUD. THUD. Three more containers slid over the side of the freighter. He found his voice, and screamed as he pushed. Harder. Harder. *Thirty-three seconds.* Edison was just then realizing that he knew pretty much nothing about calculations, and most likely, the "point-of-no-return" had already come and gone. *Thirty seconds.* He drew on every bit of reserve strength his body possessed as he willed the jet streams of water up from the falls to lift the freighter. He even pushed for the falls to reverse their flow. *Twenty-six seconds.* The blood rushing through his veins burned like fire, providing he still had blood. The bow of the freighter never rose ... but ... it was also no longer dropping. Edison had managed to halt the fall of the great ship. *Twenty-two seconds. YES!*

The hull of the freighter creaked, and the sound rung in his ears like nails sliding down a chalkboard. A new thought crept into his consciousness. *Could the ship break in half?* Once again, fear and panic began to surface. But the feeling was nothing compared to what he was about to witness. As he hovered below the freighter, the force of the surrounding falls flowed up through him. Fighting not only the weight of the ship, but gravity itself . . . his eyes began to wander.

On the other side of the council circle, overwhelmed by the ranks of the clay soldiers, Lyvx and the trees were brought down. Branches bent and broke under the rock hard fists of their attackers. Flattened in the depression of a large footprint, was the bright yellow mane of the dandelion-man. The once vivid and expressive plant was now trampled and motionless. Not far from the trampled dandelion-man Edison could see the soil beasts ripping and tearing large portions of leaves and foliage from the shrub creatures. Powerless to help, he turned his head and looked away. But just as he did, a new sight caught his attention. It made him wish he had shut his eyes and not turned his head. Apparently, another disadvantage of hovering high above a submerged island, under a 50,000-ton shipping freighter, is that you have a great view . . . of everything.

Directly below Edison, on the shore of the island, bound tightly by the dark, green coils of the vine snake was Ellie. And towering menacingly above the helpless, young girl was the Evil Viv. Vivian raised her bubblegum, pink painted claws high above her head, and slammed them down into Ellie. The little sister didn't even move. It was like beating a sack of potatoes. A lump formed in Edison's throat. And even though a dozen more containers fell from the freighter to lighten the load, the weight on Edison's shoulders slowly got heavier and heavier. Once again, the bow began to tip.

He was determined not to break, to not let the sacrifice of his new friends be in vain. He fought the fatigue, and did his best to ignore the pain. But the boy's will alone was not enough to lift the freighter. Slowly his vision started to blur. The bow tipped down several inches. He was still pushing, his limbs numb from the pain, when the blurred image of the freighter's hull dissolved into blackness. After all the battles and sacrifices he endured to get to this point, THIS was how things were to end? He would never attend a Friday night football game, a prom, a college party, or a wedding. And he would never have a family to call his own. He was reduced to the role of a spectator in his own body, and could do nothing but watch it go limp and fall. In a flash, the blackness that embraced him turned to a chalky, white light. And despite the grief and remorse he felt, he couldn't help but notice that things were playing out exactly how they described them on TV or in the movies. *Isn't the white light supposed to be at the end of some long tunnel? And for how bright the light shone, why am I so cold?* And then there was a voice, which was every bit as commanding, wise, and comforting as one would expect in such a situation.

"Young man, you and I need to talk."

The cold increased and the bright, blinding light slowly faded to darkness. *Aw, come on! I haven't been that bad. I don't need to go there,* was Edison's final thought.

"Humpf, I think he's fallen asleep?"

As usual, Edison missed all of the good stuff. The pain and fatigue were too much for his body to handle. At the height of the battle he had drifted off to sleep, passed out actually, and missed seeing the giant hand of an Ice Giant reach out from the falls and catch his falling body. Several more Ice Giants then swept in like the Calvary. They easily raised the freighter up and away from the falls, flattened the clay soldiers, scattered the soil beasts, twisted the vine snake in a few knots (a few more than needed actually), subdued a rather stubborn young girl (Vivian), and then tended to Lyvx, the trees, and the scrub creatures. The mediator stepped down from her podium, returned all of the crystals to their rightful owners, and then . . .

"I missed the vote?!?!"

Ellie shrugged. She was seated next to where Edison had been sleeping. "Yeah, you've kind of been asleep for a while."

"What year is it?"

"Not that long."

"I'm not blue anymore?"

"Correct," Ellie explained, "you're still kind of made out of the water essence, but when you relax you turn back to your 'normal' state. See, look." She lifted her fleshy pink hand, and with a flip of her wrist, it turned dark green and firm like a twisted mesh of rose stems. Her hand now resembled the plant essence that had bonded with her body. She waved her hand again and the flesh returned. Edison cringed a bit and looked down at his own fleshy hand.

"Huh? Oh, how's Viv?"

Ellie rolled her eyes, "oh, I'm fine thanks for asking."

"What?" Edison was not awake enough to grasp Ellie's sarcastic remark.

"Vivian's fine, back to her normal, obnoxiously, beautiful self."

"Is she still . . . evil?"

"No more than usual."

"Oh, well . . . I guess that's good."

"Yeah, Henry convinced the soils to stop possessing her. Actually threatened or intimidated them might be a better way to-"

"Henry?"

Ellie sat back on her heels. So much had happened while Edison slept, she had completely forgotten all about Henry. Well, not really forgotten. Since his arrival, everything had pretty much revolved around him. So much so that it was hard to remember that Henry hadn't been here the whole time. "Hmmm, do you remember when we first met?"

"When you catapulted me out over the falls," there was a bit of resentment in Edison's tone.

"Yeah, well . . . it seemed like a good idea at the time." Ellie continued, "and do you remember the giant iceberg you blasted."

"The iceberg YOU told me to blast!"

"Yeah, my bad. Anyway . . . Henry, was that iceberg you-"

"We."

"We blasted."

Edison thought back to that moment in the water where he discovered his new water powers, and how, with Ellie's tutelage, he blasted and sunk the iceberg. And he also thought of the poor face he saw in the ice as it slipped under the surface of the cold water. A gulp formed in his throat. "Henry was THAT iceberg?"

"One of the Ice Giants actually . . . the Earth's seventh essence."

"Wow, he must be pissed!"

"No, not at all. He's really cool actually. Ha! . . . no pun intended. Anyway, he completely understands and he isn't mad at all. Apparently that nasty, little root man . . . Twig, does stuff like this all the time. Lying to us, messing up the vote, setting the vine snake on us, trying to wipe out the human race . . . he really is quite nasty."

"So are you OK?" asked Edison. *Finally!* Ellie smiled. And it wasn't just because of Edison's inquiry; it was because she could tell that it was sincere. It takes Edison a while for things to sink in, but eventually just about everything does.

"Yes, thank you. I am alright, considering I'm now half-plant . . . or maybe even three-quarters-plant?" Ellie wondered.

"So then am I," Edison paused and looked down at his hands, "half-water?"

"Well . . . actually, when you were born, you were like 78% water, all babies are. And the average adult male's body is like 55-60% water. So, I'd guess now you're like . . . I don't know . . . 80-90% water? So . . . meet the new you!" Ellie, did her best to smile and put her own glass-half-full spin on things, "And I'm a new me, and Vivian is . . . a new Vivian, but still beautiful and annoying."

Edison sat up and let his eyes drift. They were seated in a patch of soft grass, just beyond the sand of the shoreline. The sound of the falls, which surrounded the submerged island, rumbled in his ears like distant thunder. But now the sound was much more soothing. Kind of like one of those atmospheric CDs you can buy in a department store, or hear in an upscale salon. Not that Edison had ever been in an upscale salon. A gentle breeze blew across the beach. And all along the jungle's edge, the leaves of the trees rippled like ocean waves. It made Edison think about the kind tree that befriended and even protected him and Ellie. The last time Edison saw Lyvx he was twisted and smashed like a tree that had been uprooted by a strong storm. "Lyvx?"

"Oh, he's fine. A few broken branches, but he said they'd grow back and he'd be as good as new in six or seven years. He also wanted me to tell you 'hello' and 'good-bye', and that he was sorry he couldn't wait until you woke up. Something about a far walk home, and then something cryptic about meeting us on the road to our next adventure or something?" Ellie made a face and shrugged. Edison was only half listening, so he missed the part about 'our next adventure.' He'd just thought about something, or someone actually, and he didn't want it to slip his mind. So instead of listening, he was just nodding. And repeating what he wanted to ask, over and over again in his mind so he wouldn't forget it. And then Ellie finally paused.

"Sorry about your little weed guy . . . I saw him smashed pretty go-" Before Edison could finish, the little dandelion man ran up onto Ellie's shoulder and perched like a pirate's parrot. He stuck out what might have been his tongue and gave Edison something of a raspberry. "Nice to see you too. So . . . how was the vote?" Edison had delayed re-asking the question, because he was afraid of the answer. To have gone through all of this trouble just to be judged once more, and found unworthy was too much to bear.

"Oh yeah, the vote . . . sorry, I should have told you right away. They postponed it . . . for five years."

"Really? How did you get them to do that?"

"Actually . . . it was you."

"Me?"

"Yeah, well . . . I guess it was you at first and then us . . . me, you and Vivian. Turns out there has never been a merging of the essences and humans, and everyone's curious to see what's going to happen next. SO . . . they gave us five years to try and do something positive."

"Like what?"

Ellie shrugged, "who knows . . . we'll figure that out later. But hey, we've got super powers now. So I'm sure it won't be that hard for us to do SOMETHING positive." Before Ellie had a chance to elaborate, she turned away from Edison. The distant rumble of the waterfalls was changing. Edison turned and saw that the splashing of the falls was lowering, and the level of the shallow water surrounding the submerged island was slowly rising. The shoreline was disappearing.

"Time to go." Ellie stood up, dusted off her knees, and extended a helping hand toward Edison.

"Edison! Get your butt down there and help with those crates!" shouted Captain Ralph.

"I'm coming I-"

"Gads boy, you're not done with that deck yet! Move 'yer butt or I'll give ya' a good boot to get jump started!"

Edison sat back on his heels and threw a sponge down into a bucket of black water. As he turned to yell back, his eyes caught Ellie's sympathetic gaze. She was sitting with her family, who was frantically pleading for everyone onboard to help scan the water. The adults were now awake and the last thing any of them remembered was the giant wave hitting the boat and sweeping Ellie and Vivian's grandmother overboard.

"Get the molasses out of yer' boots boy!" And for Edison, life was once again delightfully awful. Edison wanted to shout back, but he bit his lip instead. He figured it would only make matters worse, and his stepfather, Captain Ralph, would only end up embarrassing him even more in front of his new friends. So he muttered something under his breath and went back to scrubbing the deck.

Vivian grabbed Ellie's arm and stopped her before she could walk over to Edison. But it wasn't to save her sister or Edison from anything, it was to share the excitement of her new discovery. "Oh my God El, look! I can change my shoes! Lookie, lookie!" Ellie looked down at Viv's feet. On her foot was an open-toed, tan, leather sandal. Vivian wiggled her foot, and with a dark-brown-soil-shimmer, her sandal turned into a hot, pink sneaker. Below her new footwear, several flecks of dirt fell to the deck. "Oh my God! I bet I can do this with my entire wardrobe!" Ellie rolled her eyes as she stood up and walked over to Edison.

Ellie wanted to say something that might offer some sort of comfort, but all she could keep thinking was, *wow, it really does suck to be you.* So she didn't say anything at all.

"You know what . . . I'm done," Edison sat back and stared off into the watery horizon.

"Done?" Ellie asked.

"Yeah, I'm done. With all of this," Edison lifted up the black smelly sponge in his hand for Ellie to see. Ellie winced when the smell of the fish guts hit her nose. "I can't go back to this . . . I won't. Heck, you said it yourself . . . we've got super powers now. So, I'm done. Done with my stupid smelly bait bucket, done with this stupid boat, and done with all of these stupid, sucky foster families. " He dropped the sponge, used a small dry corner of his dirty t-shirt to whip away the tears forming at the corner of his eyes, and stood up.

"Edison, I-" Ellie reached out to touch his arm, but missed as he started to walk away. Edison walked over to a section of the deck that was empty of people, and turned back toward Ellie.

"I'm sorry . . . goodbye. And don't worry . . . my life already sucks, so it couldn't get any worse . . . right? "

Goodbye?

The boat dipped down to the left as a large wave rolled up over the side and splashed across the deck. Edison disappeared into the lake water as it ran across the deck and off the other side of the boat. It all took Ellie by surprise, and by the time she realized that her new friend was running away, he was gone . . . perhaps for good.

"What the -ell was that!" Captain Ralph yelled out.

"Another big wave!" yelled one of the passengers.

Ellie frowned. Vivian didn't even notice.

"The bait boy, where's the bait boy?" another passenger called out. Ellie thought Edison would have been amused to hear that his absence was noticed so quickly, most likely there was grunt work that needed to be done.

"I think he fell over!"

Ellie lowered her head and walked to the bench where her family was seated.

"I don't see 'em!"

Ellie wasn't quite sure what she heard the Captain grumble. But she could tell he was annoyed that he had to stop the boat and come down from his chair. She heard him swear as he waddled past her. Ellie had hoped that she, Edison, and Vivian really would have that 'next adventure' Lyvx teased about, but even at such a young age, she was old enough to know

117

that sometimes things don't work out the way you want them to. She looked out at the lake water and whispered to herself, "Goodbye, Edison."

"What did you say?" asked Vivian.

"Nothing," Ellie answered, "nice shoes." Vivian smiled as Ellie shook her head. Edison was gone, and she couldn't blame him for leaving.

"What's that?" a passenger yelled out.

"I think I see him!"

Ellie jumped up and ran over to the other side of the deck. A small crowd had gathered on the starboard side of the boat, and she had to wiggle her way through them to reach the railing. "Oh my-," Ellie couldn't believe her eyes. "Grandma!"

Floating in the water, a mere twenty yards from the boat, was Ellie's grandmother . . . and Edison. "Oh thank heavens for this young boy. He saved me. He saved my life!" the grandmother yelled up to the ship.

"Grandma?" Vivian appeared at the railing next to Ellie. "Mom! Dad! Come here . . . the bait boy rescued Grandma!" Because she was focused on him, Ellie noticed Edison had cringed, when Vivian called him 'bait boy.' She also noticed her grandmother had a very firm hold on Edison, and that he was trying to wiggle free. Edison looked more like a prisoner than he did a rescuer. And Ellie's grandmother didn't release her vice-like grip on him until they were both onboard the boat.

As soon as they were back on deck, Edison tried to slink off to the back of the ship. Ellie's grandmother quickly grabbed him before he got away.

"Not so fast young man." Edison marveled at the strength of the old woman's grip. It was definitely not the elderly grip of a gray haired woman who had spent the last two days adrift in the middle of Lake Superior. "Captain! This boy should be rewarded!" Ellie's grandmother proclaimed to everyone onboard.

"The bait boy?" Vivian questioned.

"Hush dear, name calling is an ugly trait," her grandmother added. "Oh, Captain!"

"Uh, yeah . . . rewarded. As soon as we get back" Captain Ralph stammered.

"No, this instant I believe," Ellie's grandmother was the type of woman who didn't need a microphone when addressing a crowd. She was, after all, a retired sixth grade history teacher. And she was the woman whom Ellie was named after. She spoke directly to the Captain, "He is your foster son, is he not?"

"What? Uh . . ."

"Speak up please, I'm too old to guess about your mumblings." Ellie smiled, as she watched her grandmother put the Captain in his place.

"Yes," the Captain even straightened his posture a bit when he answered. "Yes ma'am, he is."

Boy was I wrong about this not getting any worse, Edison thought.

"Well then, I think that as a reward," a small hush fell over the crowd on the boat. "I would like to take over your duties as guardian of this young hero."

"What?" Ellie's entire family spoke in unison. Edison's jaw dropped.

"Hero?" muttered Captain Ralph. He was blindsided by the old woman's request.

"Well, young man . . . what do you say? Are you ready to put your days on this fishing boat behind you?"

"Hell yeah!" Edison shouted.

"Mind your language."

"Sorry ma'am. Heck yeah!"

"Yes will do. Now, if someone would be so kind as to get an old woman something to drink, I am parched. I trust you won't be running off anywhere?" Ellie's grandmother gave Edison's arm another tight squeeze.

"No ma'am."

"Excellent," Ellie's grandmother gave Edison a friendly wink. "Now how about that drink? Geez, you wouldn't want an old woman to dry up waiting for this kind of hospitality!" Edison, Ellie, and Vivian all exchanged looks, and shared the same thought, *what the heck is going on?* "Here Edison, be a dear and put this with my things." Ellie's grandmother took off her wet windbreaker and handed it to Edison. When he took it, he noticed that there was another soaked cloth underneath. As

Ellie's grandmother walked away, Edison pulled a wet, crimson red robe out from under the old woman's windbreaker.

"The mediator?" It wasn't the first shared moment Edison, Ellie, and Vivian had had. And it wasn't going to be the last. Edison went to say something else, but just as he did he noticed the movement of the boat. The rocking up and down motion. The uneven side to side swaying. And then Vivian noticed the greenish color of Edison's face. Vivian screamed, Ellie smiled, and Edison . . .

"Eeeeee!"

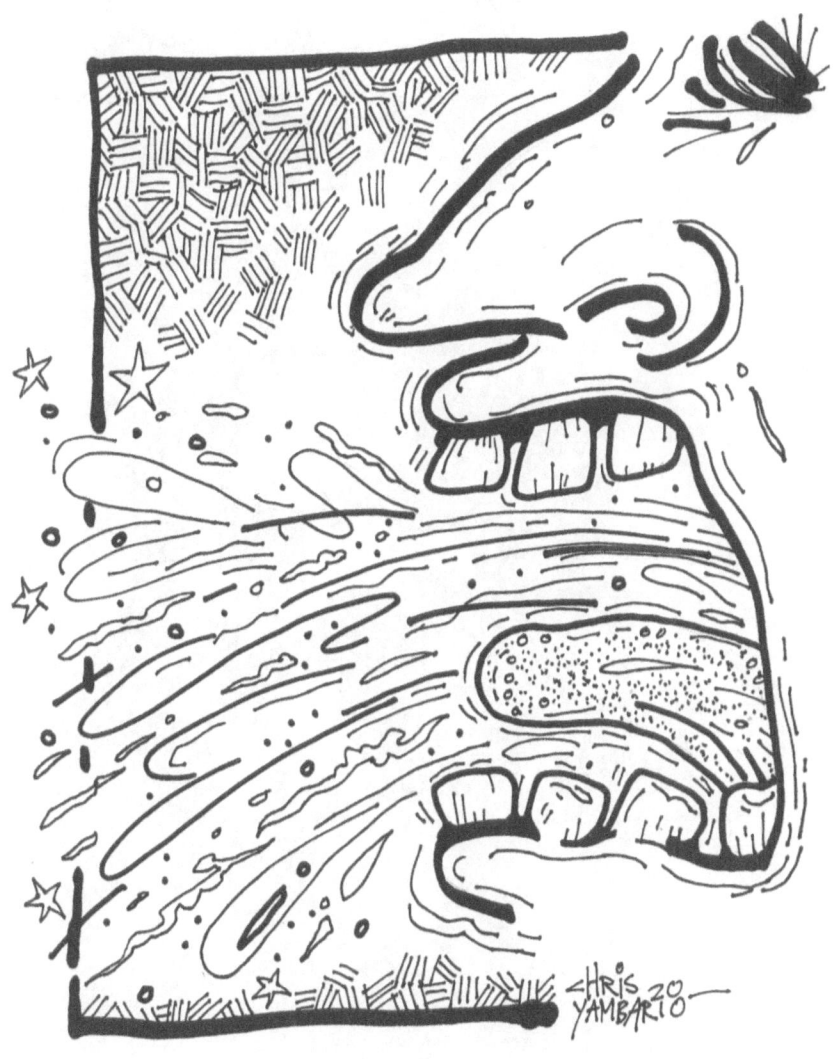

Ellie looked up at the face of her elder sister.
It was hard to tell which shone brighter, Viv's golden hair,
or the twisted and wicked crescent of her menacing grin.

Pin-up by:
Robert Atkins
Venom, X-Men, G.I. Joe, Snake Eyes, Amazing Spider-Man

From the graphic novel *The Field on the Edge of the Woods*, also by this author.
Available as a digital download on the **CLOUD9COMIX** app.

Earthlings, The Illustrations & Illustrators:

Robert Atkins – At first Robert's picture may seem out of place. He's one of the many examples of the talented and genuinely nice artists I've met sense I started writing and working in comics. So very cool to meet and even get to know all of these artists, and for Robert, it was an honor because he's already so busy with a number of different projects. His G.I. Joe work is my son Gavin's favorite. Robert is so busy in fact, that while he did say yes and drew an amazing piece for me . . . he kind of got mixed up and drew it for the wrong book. ☺ The image he drew is from *The Field on the Edge of the Woods*, a graphic novel I've written. Never really had the nerve to tell him though . . . until now I guess. *His works include: G.I. Joe, Venom, X-Men, Spider-Man.*
robertatkinsart.com

George Broderick Jr. - Every time I look at George's illustration, I like it more and more. His ability mix so many emotions in his artistic style is stunning. Edison and Ellie look so cute but the sad face of the ice giants sinking into the water makes me want to cry. Too cool. *His works include: Bozo the Clown, Speed Racer, Christmas Eve, Suicide Blonde, El Mucho Grande*
georgebroderick.com

Ron Frenz - I grew up idolizing, filling my daydreams, and copying his work in the Amazing Spider-man comics before I even know people actually drew them. It's like a dream come true to have him add an illustration for this book. He did an amazing job of capturing the vibe and attitude of the one of the books most memorable characters.
His works include: The Amazing Spider-man, G.I. Joe, Superman, Thor, Spider-Girl

Lewis Jones – His artwork literally oozes the youthful energy and fun spirit of the adventure I tried to write. I loved his image of Edison blasting a jet of water so much I put it up front on the title page. And he's just as energetic as his art, I asked him if he'd like to do one illustration and he send me three! *His works include: Infinity, Earthlings*
cloud9comix.com

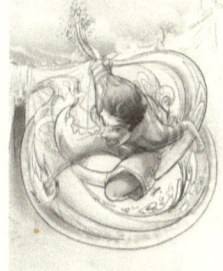  

Glenn Klimeck – I'm not sure if it's the years he's spent working in a comic book shop, literally submersing himself in storytelling art, or a honed craft, but his illustration of the vine snake bursting through the waterfall jumps of the page. *His works include: Fugitive Comics*

Terry Moore – I'm in awe of what Terry and his lovely wife have been able to do in the world of self-publishing. The stories and worlds he's created for his readers, the "Terry-verse", rival Tolkien and Rowling's. Honored to have such and incredibly talented and nice person help me create the world of Earthlings. *His works include: Strangers in Paradise, Rachel Rising, Echo, Runaways, Spider-man Loves Mary Jane*
terrymooreart.com

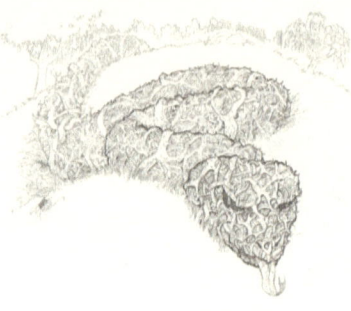

Gary Morgan – The first time we met, I watched him quick draw a fairy on a bar napkin. It took him five seconds and it looked awesome! It would have taken me an hour. As with the other artists, he had the freedom to draw whatever image (from the book) he wanted to. It was fun to see what he picked. *His works include: The Field on the Edge of the Woods, Henry, The Christian World of the Hobbit, Pants on Ants*
gmorganart.com

Loran Skinkis – A good friends, veteran marine and an amazing talent that the world has yet to discover. His image of Lyvx running with Ellie and Edison is one of my absolute favorites. And to see his creepy image of the root man drawn in a completely different style, speaks volumes about his talents as an illustrator. *His works include: Electric Owl, The Field on the Edge of the Woods, Burgh-Man, Star & Stripes*
skinkis.com

Kristoffer Smith - Besides telling what I hope is a really fun story for readers, the other joy of working on this book, has been seeing how different artists have visualized Earthlings. Kristoffer is another of those talents. *His works include: Blue Water comic's Black Eyed Peas & Lady Ga Ga, NinjaFace*
Kartprod.com

Mihailo Vukelic – His ability to take a story, or script, and breathe life into it is amazing. When I look at his image of the submerged Island, I can literally hear the rushing sounds of the waterfalls. A beautiful cover image, and fun to see that people have taken it and created a free roam online world from it. *His works include: Jimmy Palmiotti's Back to Brooklyn, Worm in the Blossom, hundreds of tattoos*
ice9tattoo.com

Geoff Weber – Where Loran did a great job of capturing the creepy side of Twig's personality; my cousin Geoff nailed his evil side. It's no wonder, we both grew up drawing Masters of the Universe characters and redrawing Iron Maiden album art.

Chris Yambar – One of the most diversely talented and interesting people I've ever met. While something of a rebel riser by birth, he even apologized for drawing what he did for the book. I couldn't have loved it more, and it inspired me to change the ending of the book. If you ever see him at a show, be sure to make time to talk to him . . . a lot of time. *His works includes: Mr. Beat, Bart Simpson Comics, Popeye, El Mucho Grande, Suicide Blonde, Spoongebob Squarepants*
yambar.com

About the author: Michael "Frick" Weber is an Emmy award winning commercial and sports television director / producer / editor. While he has written and produced several graphic novels and comics, *Earthlings* is his first novel. He lives in Pittsburgh, Pennsylvania with his amazing kids, wonderful wife and spectacular family. There are at least another dozen stories fighting to get their way out of his head, so he'd love to hear what you think about the one in your hands.

Find him on Facebook at: Michael Frick Weber, Films and Comics or The Field on the Edge of the Woods